THE HUNGUR

CHRONICLES

Samhain 2024

Edited by:
TERRIE LEIGH RELF
&
ROBERT BELLAM

THE STAFF OF THE HUNGUR CHRONICLES

EDITOR: Terrie Leigh Relf
ASSOCIATE EDITOR: Robert Bellam
WEBMASTER: H David Blalock

Cover art "Forest Vampire" by Sandy DeLuca
Cover design by Marcia Borell

Vol. III, No. 2   November 2024
The Hungur Chronicles is published semiannually on the 1st day of May and November in the United States of America by Hiraeth Publishing, P.O. Box 1248, Tularosa, NM, 88352. Copyright 2024 by Hiraeth Publishing. All rights revert to authors and artists upon publication except as noted in selected individual contracts. Nothing may be reproduced in whole or in part without written permission from the authors and artists. Any similarity between places and persons mentioned in the fiction or semi-fiction and real places or persons living or dead is coincidental. Writers and artists guidelines are available online at www.hiraethsffh.com. Guidelines are also available upon request from Hiraeth Publishing, P.O. Box 1248, Tularosa, NM, 88352, if request is accompanied by a self-addressed #10 envelope with a first-class US stamp. Editor: Tyree Campbell.

Support the First Amendment and the Small Independent Publishers! Remember, our right to publish is your right to read.

Contents

Features
6   Editors' Notes

Novelette
44   The Tears of the Pontianak by Jim Mountfield

Stories
14   A Case of Taste by Duncan Shepard
28   Prosperity Rick by Francis W. Alexander
37   A Dream Too Far by Gary Davis
69   Where the Stars Don't Shine by Robert Allen Lupton

Article
91   Why *Dracula* Rises Forever Undead by Denise Noe

Poetry
12   The Light Before Dawn by Gary Davis
36   Cold Comfort by Bill Sinyard
59   Amalthea by Terrie Leigh Relf

Sabit the Sumerian

a novella by Tyree Campbell
inspired by the Epic of Gilgamesh!

Cursed and banished to the dung-filled streets of Uruk by the king for whom she was once a companion, Sabit must now sell herself in order to survive. Near starving, and bearing the mark of the *lillu*, or vampire, she is plagued by dreams of the ancient ones who dwell beyond the mountains of Elam.

Sabit meets a girl around her own age, a kind girl with brilliant blue eyes, who asks what no other woman has ever asked: "What are you selling?" That night, Sabit's new friend comes to her in a dream, asking for that which cannot be taken, but freely given. The girl is Shala, Daughter of Ereshkigal, Goddess of the Underworld. Vampire.

Thousands of years pass. One night, Sabit, now known as Adrienne Bouchard, meets a man in a park, and her life is irrevocably changed once more. His name is Ian Cullen, a recently widowed archaeologist, with a young daughter auspiciously named Shala.

When the Daughter of Ereshkigal returns, she commands Adrienne to make a choice: Kill or turn Ian and his daughter. How will she choose? Will Adrienne sacrifice herself for two humans? Are they nothing but cattle after all?

https://www.hiraethsffh.com/product-page/sabit-the-sumerian-by-tyree-campbell

A Note from Your Editors, Terrie Leigh Relf and Robert Bellam

Hungur Chronicles, Issue Six

November 1, 2024

A Note from Your Editors . . .

Welcome to the sixth issue of *Hungur Chronicles!* We certainly hope you enjoy reading this issue as much as we did curating it. There's also an historical article along with some thought-provoking art to inspire your creativity (and yes, your curiosity).

Here's to vampires of all ilks, the stranger the better!

(And yes, the King's English is welcomed here.)

—Terrie Leigh Relf, Lead Editor

—Robert Bellam, Co-Editor

Acknowledgements:

Amalthea was originally published in 2016 in Space & Time

The Wolves of Glastonbury
by Edward Cox & Terrie Leigh Relf

What happens in Glastonbury stays in Glastonbury—even if it means the end of one of humanity's longest alternate lifelines. The hunt is on for Claire and Ethan . . .

https://www.hiraethsffh.com/product-page/wolves-of-glastonbury-by-terrie-leigh-relf-edward-cox

Blood Sampler
By David Lee Summers & Lee Clark Zumpe

Two of the finest minds in the genres have amalgamated their resources and imaginations to come up with some of the gothiest and goofiest vampire flash fiction this side of Bucharest. David Lee Summers, of *Tales of the Talisman* and *Heirs of the New Earth* fame, and Lee Clark Zumpe, mild-mannered reporter for a daily metro-Floridian newspaper, take you on a journey through tales that fit everywhere between Type O positive and Type AB negative. With a kickin' cover by Laura Givens and detailed illustrations by Marge Simon, *Blood Sampler* is a must-read even if you don't care for the suckers.

Type: Anthology – vampire – flash fiction

Ordering Link:

https://www.hiraethsffh.com/product-page/blood-sampler-by-david-lee-summers-lee-clark-zumpe

Lost Dreams Bookshop
By James W. Bullard

The old bookshop has been around before people can remember. An aging caretaker is finally being replaced and the new manager realizes the shop itself is sentient. The bookshop survives by deriving energy from its patron's lost dreams and uses that energy to manipulate people. A series of barely interacting victims who have shopped in the store over the years are telepathically summoned to return to the shop and gather on a single day not realizing their fate is in the hands of the sentient shop.

James W. Bullard lives in Colorado with his girlfriend, his son, and a spoiled Aussie shepherd. Writing is a hobby along with watercolor painting and drinking craft beer.

Type: Novella
Audience: adults

Ordering Links:
Print Edition ($10.95):
https://www.hiraethsffh.com/product-page/lost-bookshop-by-james-w-bullard
ePub Edition ($3.99):
https://www.hiraethsffh.com/product-page/lost-dreams-bookshop-by-james-w-bullard
PDF Edition ($3.99):
https://www.hiraethsffh.com/product-page/lost-dreams-bookstore-by-james-w-bullard

The Light Before Dawn
Gary Davis

As the dying sun in the west spreads shadows
    over the tombstones,
a cold wind sweeps through, and the ancient
    marbles moan.

Then a foul miasma rises from once-hallowed ground,
a faint, misshapen orb of unearthly light and sound.

A dark, cadaverous form coalesces from eddies
    in the ether.
Sunken eyes, dendritic fingers—a most unholy creature.

This denizen of the graves, whom the earth cannot bind,
glides swiftly over the headstones, trailing vermin behind.

Flying past the iron gates, it descends upon
    a darkened town.
Windows shuttered, cobblestones silent; no one
    lets his guard down.

Careening through deserted streets, the hunger grows
    by the hour,
until a distant light is spotted in a tall, medieval tower.

A shadow of feminine shape beckons the creature
    towards the light.
It scales the nitred walls, battlements looming
    in the night.

Into the chamber of a pure maiden enters death as a lover.
It approaches her reclining form; like a bird of prey, it
    hovers.

Then outside the window rises a blazing lighted sphere.
A laser blast soon pins the creature, paralyzed by fear.

The maiden now laughs—"You thought you had me
   till dawn.
You never knew you were only my alien's pawn."

The vampire fails to quench his deadly bloodlust.
In seconds he turns from skin to bone to dust.

Author's Note: Most of the stanzas in "The Light Before Dawn" originally appeared in a poem entitled, "Gothic Night," in the magazine, *Tales of the Talisman*, edited by David Lee Summers, in 2014. The last three stanzas of "The Light Before Dawn" are new, adding an outer space alien twist to the poem's more traditional Nosferatu-style vampire theme.

A Case of Taste
Duncan Shepard

This story is dedicated to my late father, George V. Shepard, who was, and always will be, an inspiration.

Chaumont, Belgium, October 1945

While I moved inexorably through the outskirts of the somnolent town, the boom of a man's voice startled me.

"Who does she think she is, Veronica Lake?" The soldier laughed.

Ugh. I knew this hairstyle was a bad idea.

"It's a long way from Hollywood, honey," the other soldier chided.

I approached the one with the corporal's chevrons above his black and white armband.

"I'm here to visit Inspector Pierre Lussier," I said, enunciating the name sharply.

The soldiers exchanged glances before narrowing their eyes at me.

"I'm detective Airth, Military Police," I said, flashing my silver-plated badge.

The corporal recoiled and straightened his back. "Sorry, we didn't mean anything by that. Just joking around," he said, scratching the back of his neck. I felt his call within the depths of my soul. ile I

"I could eat you both for breakfast." I shot a devilish grin. I was not joking.

The corporal tittered. He pointed to a cottage half a mile up a narrow road that was flanked by a beech tree. I nodded.

Shades of deep purple painted the horizon, and the crisp autumn air filled my lungs. I walked along the dirt road as the clouds descended from the sky and settled in swirls around me.

In the distance, the low hum of military aircraft rumbled, shattering the serene silence. No doubt they were practicing for the next war; some things about men never change. The closer I got to the small house, the greater my nervous anticipation grew.

Emerald vines covered the cottage, as if mother nature's veins pumped life into it. The thatched roof somehow survived the war. The windows were shuttered, but I found the entrance unlocked.

The oak door creaked as I opened it. My nostrils filled with a sickly-sweet smell and my hunger ached. Out of my peripheral vision, a flicker of candlelight caught my attention. I walked through the drawing room into the parlor.

Pierre was hunched over a worn escritoire, studying photographs. I cleared my throat.

"Pierre," I said. He turned and his gentle face brought a flood of memories with it.

"My darling, Elsie. Has it really been since the summer of '36?" He asked with his charming French accent.

An instinctive smile played upon my lips as I removed my olive-drab overcoat and straightened the sides of my lavender bodice.

"I'm on R & R," I said, self-consciously explaining why I wasn't in uniform. "I felt an urgent call from you . . . is it one of *us*?"

"Let's not spoil our reunion by rushing into business." His eyes crinkled, returning my smile. "You're beautiful as always. Ah, and what a lovely necklace. I wonder who gave that to you?" Pierre raised his eyebrows and then winked.

I hoped he would notice I wore it.

"Drink?" He offered a koetsiersglas filled with dark red liquid. My temples pulsed. I sat in a velvet cushioned chair and sipped the ruddy brew. "Tasty heme, pig's blood?"

"Lamb's actually. Pardon my impertinence, Elsie. I wish this was a social call but I'm afraid it's not. I sensed you were near enough to help." He went back to the photographs on the escritoire.

I felt compelled to share what I'd been up to since I last saw him. "I've been assisting with logistics in La Louvière. You'd never believe how often some expensive piece of equipment goes missing." I took another sip. "It's a strange feeling to be paid for work like this . . . slowly society has realized women have brains, too. I'm beginning to enjoy a freedom you've had far longer."

Pierre bobbed his head. "I'm glad you can help me in an official capacity now, even if you're off duty . . . it's about time the world saw your value." He held up the photographs. "This town believed unnatural death was behind them when the war ended. Look at these; her name is Hettie Mertens."

I stared for an endless instant. The sting of witnessing premature death was always there, even after all these years. The photos showed a young woman sprawled out under a hedge. Her skin was pallid, and her face was twisted into a grotesque expression. *Poor Hettie.*

The suffocating feeling of guilt washed over me. I only continued to live because of the anomalous, mutated form of vector-borne porphyria I received from a plague mouse. At first, after recovering from the initial illness, they thought I had a serious case of anemia. Then they grew old and died while I didn't.

"If one of us did this, *they* were clumsy," Pierre said.

I snapped back to reality. "It could also mean they don't care about hiding evidence," I offered. "Can we see the young lady?"

Pierre grimaced. "I've already examined her, but we can go down to Dr. Dierickx's practice. He's holding her before burial."

I set my glass in the wooden stand on a side table and swung my overcoat over my shoulders. Pierre grabbed a small silver flashlight, placed his black bowler on, and opened the door. Darkness fully engulfed the small town and the trancelike chirping sounds of nighttime critters surrounded us.

As our boots echoed in unison, a vision of the young woman's face flashed in my mind. *Our kind know humans have been off limits for years . . . ever since the treaty of 1897 when Stoker published Dracula. Too much bad publicity.*

The brick building silhouetted ominously under the moonlight. Pierre knocked. We waited. I interlocked my fingers and shifted my weight across my legs. Pierre stood on his tiptoes, trying to survey inside.

Dr. Dierickx opened the door with a scoff. He adjusted his round, wiry glasses and glanced back at the grandfather clock.

"Do you have any idea what time it is? Why must you always come around so late, Pierre?" The doctor asked. His voice had a pleasant lilt buried behind his annoyance.

"My apologies but my colleague just arrived in town. We'd like to view Hettie," Pierre said, removing his bowler, holding it in both hands by the brim.

The doctor's gaze lingered on me. I noticed the open bottle of brandy sitting on a small nesting table in the hallway, and his glazed look. The scrutiny of his stare cut through me. I held out my hand with the slightest hint of sensuality attempting to break the tension. "I'm Elsie, my sincerest regret for disturbing you at this hour."

He rubbed his eyes, and I could see his icy demeanor buckling with my presence.

"Mademoiselle . . . follow me." He led us through a sparsely decorated room with a rocking chair placed felicitously in the corner. The stairs going down to the basement were flanked with portraits of what I assumed were family members lost to the depths of eternity.

A shiver went down my spine as a rush of cold air seeped through my overcoat.

Hettie's body lay on the table. I held my breath. The doctor excused himself. I let out a sigh and approached her with reticence.

"There are puncture marks on the neck. Crude but certainly from a creature like us," Pierre explained as we stood around her.

I brushed Hettie's thick brown curls away from her neck with my hand.

"Truth has nuances. I've been tempted to bite the forbidden flesh from time to time, but my mind overrules my urge. It's been some time since one of us broke the treaty," I said.

"There must be a few who don't have our self-control," Pierre replied.

"Hand me your flashlight?" I asked.

I aimed the light on her neck and noticed an odd reddish color. It was in stark contrast to the waxen hue of the rest of her body.

"How long has she been deceased?" I asked.

"At least twenty-four hours," Pierre replied.

"Her neck shouldn't have this tint." I noticed the area with the puncture marks was the only place that had inflammation. "Are you familiar with this type of skin reaction? I mean, when dealing with rogue members?"

Pierre inspected Hettie's neck closer. "I can't say I am."

"I've only seen this type of reaction once before, but it wouldn't make sense if we're dealing with our kind," I said, dejected. "It was a guard stationed near Harry Daghlian when he dropped the demon core."

"Manhattan Project? So, you think it's radiation?" Pierre inquired.

"Might be." Somewhere between the hollow silence of Dr. Dierickx's basement and my cluttered mind, I knew it was a radiation burn. But why? Out here in the small village of Chaumont?

"Any revelations?" Dr. Dierickx's voice echoed in the chilly room. It startled me and I stepped back from Hettie to hide the embarrassment of being caught off guard.

"Besides what happened to Hettie, has there been anything unusual in town recently?" I queried.

The doctor rubbed the top of his head before scratching his chin. "Well, something struck me as odd the other day. I can't see how it would be connected to Hettie's death."

"No matter how inconsequential you think it is, humor us," Pierre stated.

"I could've sworn I heard a German ME 262 or something like it a few nights ago. You know, one of those jets from the end of the war? It faded quickly. I just assumed it was a flashback."

"Which direction did it go?" The description piqued my curiosity.

"Probably heading South. Again, just a phantom I'd say."

"You've been most helpful. Here, I'd like you to purchase some flowers for Hettie's funeral," I handed Dr. Dierickx a few francs.

***

We left the doctor's house and walked south from the town center toward the tree line where Hettie was found. The rolling fields were limitless at night, almost like the ocean. Occasionally the glowing eyes of an owl jumped out of an overhead branch.

"The sound Dr. Dierickx heard may just be coincidental. I conducted a preliminary inspection around here last night and didn't find anything," Pierre said, levelling his flashlight to the eye-level cluster of spruces.

I recognized the spot from the photos of Hettie. There was nothing unusual about the silent trees that witnessed the horror last night. What secrets did they hold?

"There is something kind of interesting a bit further back. Just an old war relic," Pierre said.

"Can I see?" Gentle raindrops began falling and Pierre gave me a sidelong look.

"Elsie, it's really not worth our time. Let's go back to my cottage and relax by the fireplace." Pierre tried his best to persuade me to delay our investigation in exchange for romance. How could he think I'd enjoy myself with Hettie's murder on my mind?

The pitter-patter of the rain hitting the sea of dead orange and brown leaves covering the woods got louder.

I wrinkled my nose at him. "Pierre, indulge me with the relic, please?"

Pierre shrugged and a gale of wind animated the forest, allowing it to stretch its fingers. Drooping branches reached out at me as our boots crunched on the ground. While walking, I looked through the shadows, half expecting a hidden figure to jump out at me.

He lifted his flashlight to a burned-out hunk of metal with a faded white American star on the side of it.

"Carcass of an American tank. No doubt from the battle fought here in December of '44," Pierre explained.

The raindrops became smaller and eventually eased off as we stood before the derelict war machine. The sky seemed to lower with an all-encompassing blackness.

Much further in the woods, Pierre's flashlight began glistening off something. I strained to see, just as he lowered his arm.

"Pierre, illuminate that area," I said pointing in the distance.

He huffed and raised the flashlight again. We were momentarily paralyzed with surprise. "This *wasn't* here yesterday," he said.

About a thousand yards ahead, a small clearing of fallen trees coalesced around a large metallic object. Pierre's hand began shaking. Even though my throat tightened with fear, I gently offered to take the flashlight. Possessing near immortality didn't stop our reaction to danger.

"If this is an aircraft, how did this get past Allied radar?" I asked rhetorically.

As we neared the object, the iridescent nature of the surface struck me as odd. It had a distinct lack of color and every color of the spectrum at the same time. The night critters who were symphonically chirping fell silent, creating an inexplicable eeriness. I glanced at Pierre; an incredulous look plastered upon his face. His lips trembled, as if he were about to speak but couldn't get the words out. I couldn't say anything either.

The craft resembled a tea saucer flipped upside down. Four scrawny metallic legs held it off the ground. A bulbous cap sat on top of the saucer. The enormity of the ship reminded me of a Ferris wheel laying on its side. I'd estimate it was roughly 135 feet in diameter. A ray of moonlight broke through the clouds and lit a pathway under the saucer.

Pierre wordlessly offered support as we walked along. Having him by my side subdued my will to flee.

I felt a presence behind me. Something watched us.

I spun around.

Nothing.

I heard the thumping of my heart. My temples ached for sustenance, but I could go on for a few more hours before it became a necessity.

"I get the feeling whoever owns this is not one of *us*," Pierre whispered as his expression soured. He pulled out his pocket watch; ten minutes past midnight.

From the way the ship was constructed, the bottom likely spun separately from the cap. Perhaps a way to create a gyroscopic force for intense repulsion from gravity? It seemed so primitive yet futuristic. Paradoxical, much like our own existence.

A ramp from under the saucer began descending. A faint pink hue emanated from its source. Too inviting.

"Whatever attacked Hettie must be in there," I whispered.

Pierre pulled a revolver from his jacket. "*This* doesn't stop us but who knows." His fingernails whitened as he gripped the gun.

Even with my heightened sense of uncertainty, the ramp was alluring. As we ascended the ramp with haste, each step became more difficult than the previous. My legs filled with a dull burn as I fought against the incline.

Before reaching the door, we froze in place. A malodorous smell hit me like a wall.

Death.

"I recognize this scent from tending wounded on the fields of Saratoga," I said in a hushed tone.

"Antietam with the Zouaves for me," Pierre responded.

After the treaty of '97, my view of human suffering changed dramatically. I had to relearn how and what to feed on. Whoever owned this craft wasn't playing by the same rules.

We exchanged a quick glance and entered the interior. The room was pentagonal in shape with a variety of tiny, flashing lights on the walls. A large screen hung on the left-hand side of the room.

"Like a movie theater," I said.

Pierre didn't acknowledge my comment and walked over to two swivel chairs in the center of the room. There was no sign of the occupants, but my teeth began gnashing. Perhaps a reaction to something I unconsciously sensed.

I decided to find the source of the smell. My footsteps echoed across the prodigious room. A small annex on the far side beckoned me. The stench became unbearable.

I peered into the room. My stomach churned. My arms and legs stiffened.

Why?

Before me lay a pile of corpses. The dozen or so ranged in age and gender. I knelt and lifted the little hand of a child. His fingers were curled, as if clutching at the final fleeting moments of life. Tears rolled down my cheeks.

Who would do this to an innocent boy?

I studied his face. The unevenly dilated pupils of his brown eyes stared into nothingness. His blue, shriveled lips would never know the loving kiss of a partner. His life wasn't taken; it was robbed.

My sorrow boiled into rage. Revenge was something I learned to avoid but these perpetrators were unforgivable.

Without warning a loud crack reverberated and my ears began ringing. *Pierre's revolver!*

I turned to see the commotion when a bright flash of light blinded me.

Then complete darkness.

I slept in a realm where time has no governance.

\#

Pierre's coughing woke me. Everything was blurry. I blinked until some semblance of clarity emerged. My temples throbbed with pain. I tried to lift my arm to massage them but couldn't. I looked down and saw two tight black straps crisscrossing across my chest. I was in one of the swivel chairs. My arms were restrained to the sides.

My neck hurt, as if it had been burned by the ultraviolet light of the sun. A figure dragged Pierre across the room and dropped him in front of me. It was bipedal but I could tell there was something unusual about it from the way it bent over Pierre. The visible skin that stuck out of its gray bodysuit was luminous.

It turned to me. Dark red eyes sat deep within their sockets, shadowed by a protruding brow. There were no lashes. It lifted its long, slender arm at me. I flinched as it gestured with its double opposing thumbs.

"You've made us sick," the creature growled. "My lieutenant is convulsing. Tell me what is in your blood," it ordered.

Not before I get out of this chair.

The creature snorted.

"You've injured my partner. I care about him . . . let me see if I can aid him and then I'll help you." I grasped at straws, gambling with both of our lives.

There was a soulless, snake-like quality to the eyes that glared back at me.

"Are you not afraid of me?" It asked.

"I'm not like the other people . . . the ones you killed," I said, hoping it wouldn't sense the sheer terror building inside of me.

Its bluish hand reached out and the two thumbs undid a complex series of clips. The restraints released. I didn't realize how much they had been crushing me; I could fully breathe again, although my chest hurt.

"I saw the room filled with humans. Why would you do that?" I inquired.

"We need a steady supply of iron, or our cells get out of control. We've been hopping from village to village, collecting food," it said in a guttural voice filled with hauteur.

I tried to mask my disgust. "You left Hettie outside." I searched its eyes for a reaction. Nothing. "The young woman last night."

"The female. Our meal was interrupted."

I sat next to Pierre. He passed out in my arms. His neck had sustained significant radiation burns. I rubbed my own neck and felt the scars of a burn. Hopefully, they would disappear with time.

Without warning, the creature hunched over and let out a soul twisting scream. It must've been hiding its pain until it no longer could. As shark-like as this creature was, I felt a little sympathy.

"We have a rare vector-borne porphyria. We also need heme to survive." I watched it rub its abdomen. "I suspect the changed molecular structure of our blood is reacting poorly with your digestive system. Why are you here?"

The creature fell back into one of the chairs. "We are pirates from the Maffeiladia sector. We were tailing a transport full of drenarian cattle when our navigation system malfunctioned in a space tunnel. Arange and I needed nourishment, and our scanners found this planet."

"Is Arange your partner?"

"Yes, I am Capitaneus Ebyonighter," it said. The luminosity of its skin began to dim.

"I'm Elsie Airth." Ebyonighter didn't react. "I'm sure your scanners picked up iron in all different animals. Why are you feeding on humans?"

"*Taste.*"

I laid Pierre on the ground and put my overcoat under his head.

Ebyonighter continued: "We are the superior species in our sector, and we pick and choose what creatures to engorge ourselves on. We became complacent with the volume of options we have on your planet." It wore its rectitude like a medallion. "We encountered a tribe called Nazis when hunting. They fed us a steady supply of invalid warriors for our assistance in developing their flying vehicles. We worked on the Wunderwaffe but wouldn't allow them to disassemble our craft."

They must be responsible for the Foo Fighters I heard about.

"Yes, we are. When your conflict ceased, we went back to hunting in the wild. Excuse me from intruding into your thoughts but that is how I understand and speak your language."

The apology was the first trace of empathy I heard from the creature. I seized on my chance: "Then you'll know I am deeply worried for my friend's safety and need to get him somewhere to heal."

I caught a glimpse of Pierre's pocket watch. Five minutes to seven.

"I'm too weak to stop you from leaving. But please, do you have a remedy for our illness?"

"There's no cure for our ailment. You may have it now. The only way to end it is death," I said.

Ebyonighter's thin lips twitched.

Was it hunger, pain, or realization? Ebyonighter didn't answer.

I grabbed Pierre under the arms and struggled to drag him to the entrance of the ship. I took one last look at the alien before turning my full effort to extraction.

Halfway down the ramp, Pierre regained consciousness.

"You jerk, I thought I'd lost you," I said, more frustrated than worried now.

He gave a wry smile. "Guess the revolver doesn't work on those things either."

Pierre staggered to his feet once we reached the crumpled leaves.

"We're running out of time; sunrise."

"What about the ship?" Pierre asked.

"They're too sick to go anywhere right now. Our curse may have put an end to their feast."

The sleepy eyelid of the sun began lifting as we ran along the dirt road. A shadow from Dr. Dierickx's brick building transformed from ominous to hopeful as it pointed the way to Pierre's cottage.

Rays began to shine on the door as we closed it. We were now confined to the house; the freedom of night gave way to the jail of day.

Pierre unbuttoned his shirt and collapsed into the velvet cushioned chair.

"Next time you need help on a case, maybe move my name to the back of your queue," I teased. "I don't know if the aliens will get over our ailment but I'm glad we got a little justice for Hettie. There were remains of other people on that ship . . . "

"I can safely say there are things in the shadows far more frightening than our kind," Pierre muttered.

I let out a deep breath that I didn't realize I had been holding.

"Should we turn the ship over to the Belgian government?" Pierre asked.

My tired mind raced.

"I don't know, Pierre." I filled my koetsiersglas with blood and savored the rush of relief it brought to my hunger. The haunting image of the young boy pervaded my conscience.

"I'm thinking about placing a call to a scientist I know at the National Advisory Committee for Aeronautics in America."

"That's a good option," Pierre said, as I handed him a koetsiersglas.

"It's just . . . only two months ago our atom bomb killed indiscriminately . . . innocent men, women, and children. Does that make us as bad as the aliens?" I asked.

"Elsie, we've witnessed that mankind always finds new and faster ways of killing. Maybe the magnitude of this war will give man pause. Perhaps the technology will be used for exploration . . . especially with the revelation that otherworldly beings are out there."

"At least it would keep those creatures away from innocents like Hettie."

The decision weighed on me. I still had my doubts, but I also didn't know when or if Ebyonighter would be

well enough to leave . . . or hunt. My finger rotated the dial on the telephone.
　　Would I be responsible for what they create from Ebyonighter's ship?
　　"Bonjour, opérateur, comment puis-je vous aider?"

Prosperity Rick
Francis W. Alexander

"Send your seed to Emmerich Buck. And I will mail you this heeeeeeeling cloth."

Those words take me back to the time I got on the Prosperity Rick Show. It all started in my childhood.

Many times, I visited Uncle Robert in his small two-bedroom home. One usually entered the side door and walked through the small dimly lit kitchen to the living room. He sat hunched over his desk facing the window, surrounded by a bookcase containing shelves of Christian dictionaries and other books.

The light-complexioned man with the mountainous muscles that he built from working on the railroad, was my hero. The words "God-fearing," made me think of Robert.

His wife, my Aunt Sylvia, was a sickly woman. She had suffered from strokes and things I had never heard of. The middle-aged woman had a habit of staring at walls or at whatever she faced. Whenever I visited, she'd greet me, ask some questions, then fall into what I now know to be a catatonic state. My mother said that Uncle Robert was sending money to Pastor Rick, hoping my aunt would get well.

One sunny June day while visiting them, the Pastor Rick Show was broadcasting from Uncle Robert's small brown RCA television set in the front room.

"Tickets for the Pastor Rick Show are going fast," the announcer said.

"Hey, Big Shot," Uncle Robert said as I sat on the couch watching the program, "You wanna be on the Pastor Rich Show?"

Boy did I! I knew it would be awesome for all my grade school friends to see me on television.

But there are always obstacles. My mother hated what she called "The fact that this grifter Pastor Rick is getting rich off of my sister's infirmities!" She did not want me to go see that "charlatan!"

Dad convinced her to let me go.

***

That day, clouds huddled together as if conspiring to keep the sun from shining. We took a morning train to Cleveland. Robert had taken me to a restaurant first. That's the place where I saw a man with red eyes. He wore a beige trench coat and as kids do, I mentioned it to Uncle Robert. He told me not to stare.

"Looks scary, huh, Thomas?" he said. "Remember. That can happen when you drink alcohol. So, stay away from that stuff when you get older. You hear?"

"Yes sir." I proceeded to eat my hamburger and fries.

The man sat across the aisle and about three tables up. As I ate, I occasionally glanced at him. He was eating tomato soup or broth. Every time I looked, he glared at me. It wasn't an Aunt Sylvia stare.

Finishing my hamburger, I saw him glowering. I looked down at my plate. Finished with my fries and Pepsi, I glanced his way. He was still staring.

"Well, Big Shot," Uncle Robert smiled. "It's time to go."

Joy overcame me as Uncle Robert paid the cashier and we walked out of that restaurant. I looked behind me to make sure he wasn't following us. He was nowhere in sight.

We walked several blocks over the cement sidewalks to the red brick theater. Past the ticket office, we moved. After giving the ticket taker our passes, we stepped through the entrance, past the popcorn stand, and up the dimly lit aisle where we found our seats.

The place was packed. Two people stood and allowed us to get to our seats. After I sat in my chair, the lights brightened.

"Are you ready for some miracles?" a man asked through the microphone.

The crowd roared.

"Then give a holy round of applause to Pastor Rick!"

The room exploded in applause. It was louder than the sound I heard in the *Godzilla* and *Ten Commandments* movies.

Wearing a white suit and red shirt with diamond-studded cufflinks, Prosperity Rick stepped onto the stage. Uncle Robert rose from his seat, and I followed his lead. I bobbed and weaved to get a view because the people in front of me were so tall, I couldn't see the pastor.

"It feels so good to have such a large flock of believers before me. Are ya'll ready to witness some Godly miracles?"

The crowd roared in the affirmative.

I took my seat when everyone else sat. The music began to play.

As the choir sang and the drums and tambourines played, I watched people rise. They danced with some folks acting like the ones in the Sanctified churches I had attended with my friend, Cliff. With their hands on their hips, big women danced as if they were intending to cave the floor in; women holding their dresses kicked the air, and men danced like conquistadors avoiding bulls.

After two songs, the audience sat, and Prosperity Rick moved to the podium. Someone yelled and I looked in that direction. That's when I saw him. Across the aisle and two rows up was the red-eyed stranger. I could swear it was the same person. A tall Caucasian person with shoulder-length black hair, he wore a beige trench coat. And his eyes were red. He turned, stared directly at me, and smiled with his lips closed. It gave me the creeps.

"Who is in need of a heeeeeeeling?" the Pastor asked.

"Me!" a male voice yelled. I turned and looked but couldn't see above the folks sitting behind me.

I watched as a thin figure stepped down the aisle on my left.

"Yes. Come, gentle sheep," Rick said. His right arm motioned to the man who walked up the stage's steps.

Two men in white suits took the man's hands and lead him to the pastor.

"What is your name, sir?" Rick asked.

"Jonathan."

"What is your ailment?" the pastor said.

"I have cancer. And it's hurting me now."

Prosperity Rick placed his right hand on the man's forehead and shouted, "I order you to heal!"

The man shivered and fell into the waiting arms of the men in white suits. My feet were prepared to run. I looked at Uncle Robert. He was mesmerized.

"It's gone!" the man said. I watched, mouth agape, as he stood, and ran down the steps.

The music boomed as the healed sheep pranced down the aisle and back to his seat.

"Who else needs healing or wealth?" the pastor asked. I didn't think the response would come from Uncle Robert because Aunt Sylvia was back in Sandusky.

"The woman in the wheelchair!" shouted Pastor Rick.

I watched as a young man pushed a middle-aged lady down the aisle on my left. When the pastor and the two men left the stage, I stood to get a better look.

After reaching the woman in the center aisle the pastor and the two men said some things to the woman.

"You cannot walk?" the pastor exclaimed.

"No," the woman replied.

"Yes, you can. You have to believe! Get up and walk!" The pastor stared at her. She did not move. The two men lifted her out of the chair. They kicked the wheelchair out of the way and her helper retrieved it.

"You. Will. Heal!" He placed a palm on her forehead and pushed. The woman fell back into the men's arms. They lowered her to the ground.

"Get up and walk!" he said.

Slowly, the woman rose. She took one step, two steps.

"I can walk," the woman screamed. "It's a miracle!" The woman slowly moved, then walked fast down the aisle. She turned and ran back to the stage. The crowd roared and the music played as she started to dance. I felt the hairs on my head rise as if affected by a rubbed comb. I stood and attempted to move past Uncle Robert. He grabbed my arm.

"Sit down, Big Shot!" he said, "It's okay. We are in a good place."

***

I could have sworn there had been over one hundred healings. According to Uncle Robert, sleep had overcome me after the sixth healing. I looked at Uncle Robert's watch and saw that we had been there for four hours. It felt very good to know the show was ending based on the host's prayer.

Although tired from sitting in those wooden chairs, I had pep in my step when we left our seats. I was going to the train station on the way home!

"Come with me," Uncle Robert said. Puzzled, I held his hand as we walked up the steps to the stage while the last of the audience headed for the exits.

"Where are you going, sir?" a man dressed in black said to my uncle.

"I need to see the pastor," Uncle Robert responded.

"The show is over."

I must see him," Uncle Robert said. His hand squeezed mine.

"The pastor is not seeing anybody else, sir," the man said.

Uncle Robert pulled the wallet from his back pocket and withdrew a fifty. "How's this?" he said.

"One hundred will do," said the man.

"No!" I shouted. Robert slapped a hand over my lips.

He pulled out a Ben Franklin and handed it to the man who then turned and led us down a dimly lit hall to the door of the pastor's dressing room. Two men stood on each side of the door.

"What is it?" someone cried from inside the room after the man knocked.

"A sheep," said the man.

We waited for what seemed like an eternity. The door opened and a shapely blond woman exited, straightening her clothes.

"What can I help you with, my good man?" grinned the pastor. He signaled for the man next to us to leave and motioned for us to come inside. Then he closed the door.

"My Sylvia is getting worse," Robert said. "I've sent you money and received prayer cloths, prayer rugs, holy rings, and other things, and they are not working."

"It also takes faith," the pastor said.

"He has faith!" I shouted. Uncle Robert covered my mouth with his huge right hand.

"Please excuse him," Robert said. "My nephew has better home training than that."

A squeaking noise erupted from a heavily shaded corner of the room. I looked in the dressing mirror and saw what looked like a mannequin or a stand sporting a beige trench coat. It began to move.

"Faith?" a voice said.

I looked in the corner.

Red eyes appeared above the stand. I had no doubt it was the man I'd seen earlier.

"Where'd you come from?" the pastor asked.

"Your soul," the man responded.

Uncle Robert grabbed my arm and we moved towards the door. I looked back and glanced at the mirror. Instead of seeing the man, I saw a trench coat with no head. From what I heard about vampires, that man fitted the description. I couldn't wait to get home and tell Cliff and the guys that I saw a vampire. But first, I had to get out of there. With Uncle Robert there, I still had no doubt I was safe.

A couple of feet from the door, we stopped. I couldn't move.

"Get thee away, Satan!" the pastor said. He tried to move Uncle Robert out of his path to the door. Unable to do that he stepped around the hulking man.

"Hank! Carlos!" the pastor shouted.

The door opened and the two men entered.

"Sit," the stranger said. The two men sat on the floor.

Still able to move, the pastor moved for the open door. It slammed in his face.

I tried to move. Couldn't. I turned my eyes to see Uncle Robert. He couldn't move either. The pastor, unable to escape, swiftly moved to the desk and retrieved some articles out of his bag.

The man smiled. Slobber streamed down both sides of his mouth.

"A vampire," the pastor said. He went into his bag and pulled out a small bottle of clear liquid.

"You said to have faith," the man said. "Your faith is money and pleasure. I can give you pleasure as you've never dreamed of having."

"Go!" the pastor said. He unscrewed the bottle and tossed its substance at the man.

"How much for the holy water?" the man asked. Most of the liquid hit the floor. Some drops landed on his pants and shoe. He snatched the bottle from the pastor and drank its contents.

"I should make you pay the laundry bill," he said.

Prosperity Rick reached into his shirt and brought out a gold cross pendant.

"Bonafide, pure gold!" the man grinned. He walked up to the pastor and ripped it off Rick's neck. He tossed it up and down with his right hand.

"Whew! Boss!" the man said, "This has to cost nearly one thousand dollars. Our master has treated you well."

The pastor shook like he had delirium tremens. It was now apparent to me that he couldn't move, either. The vampire walked up to the pastor, grabbed the shoulders, and lowered his head. With white fangs emerging from his mouth, he looked at me. Then, he sunk his teeth into Rick.

He moved, with thin streaks of blood flowing down the sides of his mouth in my direction. Suddenly, I had the urge to use the bathroom. I felt like a fly in a spider's web. At least the fly could move. Horrified, I stared at his gleaming fangs.

"Lawd, Lawd!" Uncle Robert said.

I found myself able to move. Uncle Robert could, too.

"You're evil," the man said. He moved backward, leaned down, and went into the pastor's pocket. He retrieved some money and threw it at Robert.

"God rules here!" Uncle Robert said.

Fear wearing down his face, the man backed towards the darkness from which he had come. A few seconds later, I furrowed my brow and strained my eyes to see him. No one was in the corner.

I picked up any bill I could find.

"Leave it!" Uncle Robert said. "That is stealing, and we don't steal. Now let's go!"

I threw the money back on the floor. As I walked out the door a bat flew past.

I contemplated going back to get the money. Uncle Robert grabbed my hand and whisked me toward the stage. After closing the door, I heard some rustling inside. I voluntarily walked fast because I didn't want to confront Carlos and Hank. Plus. I had to use the bathroom.

***

After that night Uncle Robert turned more to faith than believing in man. Aunt Sylvia improved to the point that she stopped staring into space. I smile whenever I think about their loving relationship.

One thing that still puzzles me to this day, is Uncle Robert shouting "Lord, Lord" in that dressing room. I asked him why he did it. He'd told me that he didn't know. "It just came out," he'd said.

I don't trust prosperity preachers nor Jim Jones type of evangelists who boast that they can heal. That incident strengthened my faith and keeps me from fearing even vampires.

Cold Comfort
Bill Sinyard

I was her first love, she said
The first in four hundred years
She said come,
and I did
She promised if I trusted
we would live forever together

Yes, she was cold, she said
but a cold kiss
is warmer than a sad life
I believed her,
I believed her power would transform me
despite the cold of her touch,
the elsewhere gaze of her pale eyes

At night, every night
a little more
A little more and I would join her forever
Forever, she said forever
I wait in the darkness and I am weaker, drained
and afraid she might sense my doubts
She promised life
a vital transformation
I invited her in and she returns
I wait
I hope and wait and,
for the first time
I am afraid
Afraid of her frozen beauty
And my weakness

A Dream Too Far
Gary Davis

Finally, Samantha was in her element; she could feel it. Singles ballroom dances were not common anymore, as most people now searched for prospective partners on dating websites and apps. As a young teen in middle school, her parents had pushed Samantha into attending a ballroom dancing class. She pouted and was reluctant at first, as ballroom dancing seemed very old-fashioned and more appropriate to her grandparents' generation. Gradually, Samantha came to master and enjoy foxtrots, waltzes, swings, and a dizzying variety of Latino movements.

Taking her time with dressing and make-up, Samantha showed up in the middle of a dance sponsored by local Fire Station No. 3, which happened to be adjacent to an ancient community center ballroom. The parquet hardwood floor was worn and scuffed but still shiny. As was her intention, Samantha walked through the door when the music and dancing had already been underway for a good hour or more. She never liked to arrive early at a large social event, which she felt garnered too much flattering attention from the opposite sex. There was a small guitars, keyboard and brass band playing up on the stage, alternating between soft rock and older pop standards.

Feeling a tad nervous at first, Samantha walked directly over to the refreshments table upon entering the cavernous ballroom. She poured herself a large fizzy cup of soft drink with ice and gulped half of it down quickly. She then sat down in an antiquated chair along the wall of the ballroom. A man soon came over to her, extended his hand and asked her to dance. "Hi. I'm Ricky. This is a great rock song, if you'd like to try it out on the dance floor." Samantha, however, made it a routine to always refuse the first one or two men requesting a dance. She looked up at him, smiled politely and replied, "Thanks, but I'm just going to sit here for a while. Have a nice evening." A second man walked over to her a few minutes later, and Samantha gave him the same dismissive reply.

Samantha looked inquisitively around the dance hall and up at the band. She then turned her eyes to the entrance door and observed a tall, dark-haired man, attired in elegant black and white evening dress, stride confidently into the ballroom. She sat straight up and patted down her blond hair. The new attendee apparently noticed Samantha out of the corner of his eye and slowly walked over to her chair. Without seeming to smile much, he bowed and proffered his hand. Samantha looked up and blushed a bit. His formal suit was very attractive and appeared somewhat overdressed for this event. As the man spoke, she thought to herself, "Three's a charm."

"Good evening, Miss. I'm Victor, at your service. May I have the pleasure of the next dance?" What formality, Samantha wondered, although coming from him, it seemed perfectly natural. "Yes, of course," she blurted out. "I'd be happy to dance with you. My name is Samantha, by the way."

"Why, that's a very pretty name as are you," Victor responded.

The two walked out towards the middle of the crowded dance floor. Victor's presence was quite commanding, Samantha thought. A waltz, the Oscar-winning movie song "Moon River," had just started playing. This was Samantha's favorite style of classic dance. Victor twirled her around like a pro. Up close, his breath felt surprisingly cold, but that was a relief given the hot ballroom lights directly above her.

Samantha and Victor followed the waltz with a foxtrot and a swing and then sat back down to talk. Samantha pointed out the refreshments table, but Victor waved his hand, saying he didn't care for anything right now. The two embarked on an animated and pleasant conversation with some physical science thrown in. Samantha's interest perked up. Samantha mentioned that she had taken several upper-level astronomy classes in college. Victor stated that he liked astronomy, too, especially watching videos about the Solar System, exoplanets, stars, nebulas, and galaxies. "I've learned so much in just a few days," he said proudly. His lips seemed thick to Samantha, and he didn't open his mouth much while speaking. Nevertheless, his voice sounded very resonant.

After another 20 minutes, the lights dimmed. The band began a romantic suite of slow dances, mostly older pop tunes. The chairs quickly emptied, and the ballroom floor filled up. Samantha grabbed Victor's hand, and they eagerly joined the dancers. She leaned in close to Victor, resting her head on his broad shoulder and closing her eyes. She was surprised at how fast her feelings for Victor were developing. This had never happened to Samantha before—such a sudden upswell of romantic attachment. She wondered why for a few seconds, but quickly suppressed any doubts about him and made her decision.

Victor and Samantha returned to their chairs, tightly holding hands. "Hey, let's go back to my condo, if you'd like," Samantha stated. "I have a nice, comfy, one-bedroom place."

"That's wonderful," replied Victor, bowing slightly in his typically formal manner. "I would be delighted."

Samantha added, "You can follow me in your car."

"Oh, that won't be necessary, since I came here by cab," said Victor. "I only just arrived in the U. S. from Spain and haven't had a chance yet to obtain a driver's license. I'm so busy in the daytime these days."

The two left the singles dance, still in full swing, and Victor followed Samantha to her black BMW. They did a passionate locking of the lips before getting in the car and driving off. After parking in front of Samantha's five-story brick condominium building, they walked upstairs to the second floor. Upon entering her place, Victor followed Samantha straight to the bedroom. The couple exchanged a little small talk, quickly shed their evening clothes, and plunged under the sheets of the queen-size bed. Their lovemaking was the best and smoothest that Samantha had ever enjoyed. Victor certainly had the perfect touch.

Samantha immediately fell into a deep dream-sleep afterwards. This dream felt like a totally new experience, a sort of sixth sense. She began "flying" rapidly beyond the Earth into outer space. She was not inside a spaceship or even wearing a spacesuit, just ordinary clothes within the vacuum of dark space. Samantha zoomed past the Moon, then past the red planet Mars. She got a breathtaking view of gas giant Jupiter with its swirling clouds and Great Red Spot. Next, she coasted by Saturn and its famous rings. She passed ice giants Uranus and Neptune, both a similar shade of light greenish blue. Samantha felt like she was slowing down as her dreamscape took her around dwarf planet Pluto, named after the ancient Roman god of death. She caught a good view of Pluto's recently discovered bright "heart" region. Otherworldly space seemed so romantic, Samantha thought within her dream. Was that Pluto heart a special message from her new lover?

Samantha's dream now launched her into orbit around Pluto. She then began descending toward the methane and nitrogen surface ices of that frozen world when she suddenly woke from her dream-sleep. Samantha slowly sat up in bed. She turned her head around and noticed that Victor had gone, although it was not quite daylight yet. He hadn't left anything behind, she thought. Samantha turned around in the other direction, however, and saw a small hand-written note next to the lamp on her bedside table. It stated, "Sorry, I have to leave early. Very busy in the day. See you again tonight, my dear. Love, Victor."

Samantha sighed and frowned. She was obviously disappointed that Victor had left so early and without saying good-bye. At least he would show up for more intense romance again tonight; that prospect delighted her. Samantha laid back down in her bed and closed her eyes. Her neck was sore and itchy. Plus, she felt very tired, sleepy, and not at all ready to get up for her workday. Maybe her seemingly endless dream-flight through millions of miles within the Solar System had worn her out. That was an interesting, strange thought. Fortunately, Samantha's job was all remote business number-checking, on a telework laptop and with few day-to-day deadlines. She was simply expected to put in a certain weekly total of work hours at any time of day or night. She soon drifted back to several hours of dreamless sleep.

After waking up again, late in the morning, and still feeling dog-tired, Samantha dragged herself into the bathroom and looked at her neck in the mirror. She saw several deep red blemishes. Perhaps Victor had given her some strong hickeys while she was dreaming. She had never received one before and didn't know what they were supposed to look like. Samantha could not bring herself to do any work that afternoon; she called in sick to her office.

Not long after Samantha had finished her lasagna and salad dinner that night, Victor showed up at the door. As usual, he bowed politely and gave Samantha a firm hug, but didn't say a lot or really open his mouth much at all. He did bring a small gift with him—a beautiful, long-stemmed red rose. Samantha put the rose inside a narrow vase with water, then offered Victor a portion of her left-over dinner items.

"Thanks, but I had my dinner earlier," he replied. "I don't really eat or drink much anyway, especially at night."

The two of them retired to the bedroom and removed their clothes. Samantha now felt weak as well as tired, but she willed herself to keep going. She gradually got into a comfortable rhythm of lovemaking. Samantha began wondering if her mind wasn't completely her own anymore, but perhaps that was just symptomatic of a new deep romance. She would think more about it tomorrow, she promised herself.

Once again, Samantha collapsed into sleep right afterwards and entered an extended phase of dreaming. She was back in outer space and now flying well beyond Neptune and Pluto, past the comets and other icy dwarf objects in the Kuiper Belt that Pluto is a part of. After zooming through this region, she passed through the outermost shell of the Solar System, known as the Oort Cloud. The few bodies that Samantha saw here were mostly comets, but lacking much of a tail because they were so far from the Sun.

Within this vivid dream state, Samantha felt a surge of isolation and loneliness. She already missed Pluto's romantic heart feature. She was passing well beyond the Solar System and surrounded by utter darkness, with the Sun itself appearing as a small distant star. Was she really headed towards anywhere? Samantha almost felt like she was drifting asleep within her own dream.

The dream began to move faster, however. Samantha was now out among the stellar arms of the Milky Way galaxy. She saw clusters of stars and huge gaseous and dusty nebulas in the distance. Samantha sensed that her speed while traversing space had tremendously accelerated. She was now zooming high above the bright center of the Milky Way. Somewhere far down, there was a supermassive black hole; she didn't think it would suck her in, however.

Within her dream, Samantha had traveled about 25,000 light-years from the Solar System. She proceeded across to the far side of the Milky Way. Traveling for another 20,000 light years, she began slowing down within one of the galactic spiral arms. Samantha now approached an alien planetary system. Up ahead, she spied a large, bluish exoplanet with an atmosphere. She continued directly towards its north polar region.

The central star of that planetary system had just set, and the sky was rapidly getting dark. She began circling over a tall, barren, craggy mountain. Samantha could see a flock of about a dozen huge, bat-like flying creatures swarming around the mountain peak. Each of their giant claws held a small, limp, humanoid-looking being. The humanoids, only about two feet in height, all looked pale and dead as their wrinkled faces came into view. The bat creatures dropped the bodies of their prey on top of a ledge a few feet below the mountaintop. Then, suddenly, the bats all swooped down to the peak itself; they simultaneously coalesced into one six-foot tall, human-like being.

Samantha gasped within her dream. The face of that tall humanoid looked exactly like Victor. He was smiling and looking up directly at Samantha within her dream. For the first time ever, she saw him with his mouth wide open, revealing four long fangs and dripping blood down his chin.

Samantha woke up. It was still pitch dark, hours before sunrise. The rose from Victor had already wilted to black. Samantha was not only feeling extremely weak and emaciated, but now she could hardly breathe. Each breath became shorter and fainter. Her chest heaved up and down with a jerky motion. Her neck was on fire with pain.

Samantha then felt a piece of paper lying next to her hand. With great effort, she lifted the paper up to her dimming eyes and read it from the moonlight coming through the window. As Samantha took her final breath, she saw what the note said: "Sorry, I had to go back home tonight. Your truly, Victor."

Strange that he never roused the lady's ire.
She dreamed too late her love was a vampire.

(Note: The two lines of poetry at the end of this story come from my previously published poem, "Dancing into Her Lover's Dream," *The Hungur Chronicles*, Walpurgisnacht, 2022.)

The Tears of the Pontianak
Jim Mountfield

ONE

It waited in the study.

Our penthouse's floorplan called the room a "study," but my wife and I had put nothing in it. We had no books to fill the shelves covering its northern and southern walls nor any big desk to place in its centre so that, sitting there, I could admire the view through the western wall, made entirely of glass. It was an embarrassingly empty space – embarrassing because it reminded me of how I didn't read (which, I told myself, was because I didn't have time to read) and how I didn't properly work (which was because I did most of my job shouting or tapping angry messages into my various smartphones). However, when the chest of drawers arrived, the study seemed an appropriate place to store it until I presented it to my father-in-law.

The study's light was off when I entered, but I could see the drawers thanks to the nocturnal light coming through the glass wall. Beyond it stood Singapore's great forest of apartment-blocks, condos, with skyscrapers in the distance.

Yet the light seemed odd. It pooled in the middle of the study, around that lone piece of furniture. It showed the rosewood doors hanging open, which surprised me because I thought I'd closed those doors earlier. It also showed the teakwood fronts of the 24 drawers inside, arranged in four columns of six, and the carvings on the teak, which depicted four trees rising up the four columns, so that the lower drawer-fronts were bisected by their trunks and the upper ones were crowded with their branches.

Simultaneously, the surrounding floor, beside the study's walls and in its corners, was dark.

I approached the chest of drawers and, without knowing why, took one by its handle and eased it forward. It belonged to the second column from the right and was maybe the third one down. Then something added to the pool of light – a pale, secondary light, emanating from the drawer. I also noticed a fruit-like odour. Looking down, I wondered for a confused moment if another gift I'd once given my father-in-law, an antique mahjong set with ivory tiles, had somehow been dumped inside the drawer. It was filled with small, white chips, scattered on a layer of red velvet –

Then I understood what I saw. The red velvet was blood. The white mahjong tiles were teeth, violently removed from someone's mouth.

Then I was no longer in the study. I was in bed, in one of the bedrooms at the far side of the penthouse. Not the master one, because my pregnant wife was sleeping in that and we'd agreed to sleep separately until our child arrived – which, if all went according to schedule, would be shortly before my father-in-law came from Shanghai. Mei said she didn't want to disturb my sleep with her night-time visits to the bathroom. From one or two veiled comments she'd made, though, I suspected that sometimes I'd disrupted her sleep recently by speaking or even crying out while I was unconscious. I had no memory of those incidents.

I grasped at the switch of my bedside lamp, then struggled from under the bedclothes and onto my feet. As I passed the room's blinds, I heard a rustling noise – rain beating on the terrace, heavy rain if I could hear it, because the penthouse was well-soundproofed. I went out into the main corridor, whose lights were left on in case Mei decided to use the big bathroom during the night rather than the ensuite one in the master bedroom, and walked to its other end. That was where the study-door was. I entered the room for real, just minutes after I'd entered it in the dream.

The light in the actual study was different. Granted, at this late hour, the towers west of our building were aglow with lights that shone from the windows of their many landings and endless stairwells. But the rain oozing down the glass's far side smeared, muffled and diminished them and this was a darker room.

While I reached for the switch by the doorway, I noticed something about one part of the glass wall. Two red beads of light hovered outside it – surely just outside it, just past the sluicing rainwater, because unlike the other, blurry lights in view, these were small and sharp. They were set on some pale, oval-shaped surface, on which I began to discern other features –

At the same time my finger pushed the switch, it occurred to me that a face was floating outside the window, a shockingly red-eyed face staring in at me. Then the study lit up. Looking through the bright light, I 46ealized the face was no longer there. It couldn't have been there. No terrace existed on the western side of the penthouse. The only solid surface beyond that glass was twenty stories below.

I'd barely got over the shock of the imagined face when I noticed something else. The rosewood doors on the chest of drawers hung back on their hinges and a drawer jutted open – second column from the right, third drawer down.

TWO

The chest of drawers had arrived the previous afternoon. Our building's management insisted that the inside of the lift, the exclusive lift that bypassed 19 stories of apartments below us and serviced our penthouse only, be draped in plastic sheeting and rubber padding during the delivery. This would eliminate any danger of the furniture's edges and corners scratching its sides. To deck the lift out like this, I had to pay the management 200 Singaporean dollars. Obviously, 200 dollars meant nothing to me, but the principle of it rankled. This city . . . Whatever way you turned, it found opportunities to relieve you of money.

The delivery-men moved the drawers into the penthouse, supervised by Mr. Lim. Before the lift-doors closed behind them, I noted how the lift-interior, with its temporary plastic and rubber surfacing, resembled a padded cell in which straitjacketed lunatics were incarcerated in old horror films.

When the chest of drawers was in the study, Mr. Lim unrolled a strip of cloth along its top. He lodged a jeweler's eyepiece in his right eye, produced a small key from a wooden box he was carrying, and inspected the bit at its end. Then he set the key in a particular position on the cloth. With maddening pedantry, he repeated this action 25 times, until 25 more keys lay along the strip. "All present and correct," he said. "A to Z." He lifted a key off the strip's end, handed it to me, and handed me the eyepiece too. "You'll see the letter in the pattern of clefts and wards. Capital A."

I squinted through the eyepiece for a minute. Finally, I made out the A, its shape lurking partly in the way the bit had been cut and partly in the moulding of the metal. "And they fit each drawer in order?"

"Yes, A is top drawer left, X is bottom drawer right. Across and down."

"And Y is the secret drawer?"

Mr. Lim crouched at the drawers' side and, from near the back, extracted a twenty-fifth drawer that was positioned vertically, not horizontally. Its keyhole was almost invisible amid the rosewood's dark-red colouring. Since it had no handle, opening it required dexterous fingers.

"And Z?"

He closed the twenty-fifth drawer. "Ah, the secret, *secret* drawer, if such a thing exists. Nobody at the auction house was able to find a twenty-sixth drawer. To make sure, they'd have needed to saw the piece open, causing it irreparable damage. But perhaps it's just a rumour. A ruse."

"Ruse?"

"The purpose of these drawers is to confound thieves. There's surely something valuable in them. But in which drawer? A thief finds your key-ring and goes through the 24 visible drawers and probably discovers things of value. But are they the *most* valuable things there? He notices another key on the ring. Another drawer, surely? He keeps looking and eventually discovers the secret drawer. But is what's inside it *truly* the most valuable item? For he's realised that there's another key on the ring. That means a further secret drawer, which must contain the most valuable thing of *all*. So he keeps searching. And searching . . ."

"And becomes obsessed? Goes mad, even? These drawers are a trap that drives thieves to obsession and madness?"

Mr. Lim chuckled. "Yes. In an unsubtle manner of speaking."

Then he bowed and held forward a slip of paper – his bill. The old antiques dealer didn't offer his services cheaply. Still, the sum requested didn't break the bank. Not *my* bank, anyway. I used an app on one of my official phones to transfer the money. A graphic accompanied the transaction, depicting it as a page being folded into a paper airplane, which then skimmed through the air to its destination, Mr. Lim's account.

He set the eyepiece on the end of the cloth, beside the final key. "You can have this for free. You'll need it if the keys ever get mixed up." Then he mused, "I never determined where this chest of drawers came from. Among the merchant's papers, there were no receipts for its purchase. Maybe it was given to him as a gift."

We walked towards the lift. Mr. Lim continued, "A very rich man, that merchant, back in colonial times. Like all sensible rich men, he kept a low profile. He avoided fame. His life was mostly secret."

I nodded. I could relate to that.

"Indeed, the only time he got publicity was when he died."

"Why?"

Mr. Lim stepped into the padded-cell-like lift. "He committed suicide. Suddenly. For no apparent reason."

THREE

Mei's voice startled me. "You're worried about it," she said behind me. "You're afraid my father might not like it."

I straightened up from it, leaving half-a-dozen drawers protruding from its front. This was the fifth or sixth time today that I'd gone into the study and on this occasion my wife had followed me. Her father not liking it concerned me, but that wasn't at the forefront of my thoughts just now. However, I went along with her, to avoid telling the truth. "You're right. I want it to impress him."

She came to my side and studied the chest of drawers uncomprehendingly. It baffled her how people like her antique-obsessed father could like old things, when to her the only things that mattered in the world were new ones – lushly, sparklingly, expensively new. As if to emphasize this, she wore a long red gown whose plunging V-neck did much to distract from the baby-bump nestling amid its pleated folds. I wondered how much the gown had cost in Paragon, or Mandarin Gallery, or whatever Singaporean money-trap she'd found it.

"Be careful," she advised. "My father has principles. One of them is that respect can't be bought. If he thinks you are trying to buy his respect with this, he'll despise you instead."

After she'd left the study again, I considered her principles. Did she really love me? Or had I, with my massive fortune, merely bought her affections just as I was trying to buy her father's respect? I went to the glass wall and gazed out at daytime Singapore. Last night's rain had given way to a day of blinding sunshine and blistering heat. The city seemed to shimmer with wealth.

Who, I wondered, was the last person who'd truly liked me? Been my friend not because of what I owned but because of the person I was?

Mo Taylor. For many years he'd been my best friend. Though in the end . . . He'd betrayed me.

I corrected myself. No, I'd believed he was going to betray me.

***

All day I kept returning to the chest of drawers, going through them, finding nothing inside their wooden cavities.

Then, when I entered the study after dark and before I switched on the light, I noticed something new. A blemish was faintly visible on one of the upper drawer-fronts – a pale discolouration hovering amid some of the branches carved on the teakwood. Somehow, this had become discernible by a strange effect of the light penetrating the glass wall, from the cityscape outside.

I forgot about the light-switch and approached the drawers. The blemish seemed to fade. It was gone by the time I touched the drawer where I thought it'd been. Puzzled, I took the handle there and pulled it back. A shaft of new light rose from its interior, into my face, and I looked down.

The hideousness of the sight contrasted with the smell accompanying it, which suggested fruit and jasmine. I didn't have to count the things filling the drawer. I knew there'd be ten. Eight fingers and two thumbs, their ends bloody and ragged where they'd been severed.

Then, again, I found myself not in the study, but in my bed. I managed to avoid crying out, remembering Mei asleep in a neighbouring room, our child inside her. I clawed myself free of the sheets and blanket and sat for a time, surrounded by darkness. The only thing piercing that darkness was a speck of light on the air-conditioning unit, which murmured in a corner.

Suddenly, as if the unit was malfunctioning, the murmur changed to a louder, more discordant sound. I realised I heard something caterwauling – screeching with grief and despair. And the sound came not from the corner at all, but from closer, from somewhere behind me. I twisted around.

I saw the eyes, bigger, brighter and redder, like two burning coals. And this time, despite the darkness, I saw more. A white face, framed by tresses of black hair that straggled onto the shoulders of a white gown. White hands, turned into claws by their long, curved fingernails. Tears glistening on its cheeks, though its mouth was stretched in a ferocious grimace and showed crooked teeth and crimson gums –

For a moment this apparition loomed on the other side of the bed from me. Then it disappeared and once again the darkness in the room was absolute, save for the little air-conditioning light in the corner. And then I forgot about my sleeping wife and did cry out.

More than that – I screamed.

FOUR

"What are you doing?"

I told her, "I thought it might be better if this is locked when I give it to your father. It's his to open and explore, if he wishes." I was taking each key and turning it in the keyhole of the corresponding drawer. This entailed much picking up of keys and locking of drawers. To Mei's eyes, I must have looked compulsive-obsessive.

"Do you feel better?"

"I'm fine," I lied. "I don't even remember the nightmare now."

"You don't? Something that made you scream like that?"

"Nope. But whatever I dreamt about, I'm sure it was just some manifestation of stress. Stress about work. Stress about . . . " I smiled feebly and patted the bulge in her tummy. "Maybe this pregnancy is making me suffer too."

She didn't appreciate my attempt at humour. Despite the extra maids I'd hired to fuss over and indulge her, and despite the state-of-the-art check-ups and treatments I'd paid for her to get at Mount Elizabeth Novena Hospital, pregnancy was a terrible ordeal for her. No man – come to think of it, no other woman either – could imagine the suffering she was going through.

We swapped a few more, desultory words before she left me alone. Only then, as she walked away, did I notice that today she wasn't in the red gown. She wore an identically-styled white one.

***

I stared through the glass wall into the shimmer of heat and sunlight, steel and concrete, money and opulence. I was good at compartmentalising things. I could put the positive things about me in a few compartments and focus only on those. I stashed the negative things elsewhere and managed to never, or only rarely, look and shudder at them. Probably that was how I'd climbed out of the gutter, risen through the ranks, made myself the man I was today. In a way, my mind was a mental equivalent of the 24, or 25 – or 26? – drawers behind me.

Now, I dared to look into a compartment, a drawer, in my memory marked: "The Last of Mo Taylor."

Another thing I was good at was acting. At one time I'd even considered doing it as a career, having starred in school plays, and ones staged by my town's amateur-dramatics group, and later in drama-soc productions at college. The acting career ultimately never happened, but my acting skills were useful to me afterwards. At heart, I'm a weakling and coward. Yet you wouldn't think that if you knew me only from my performances.

That afternoon, among some forested hills in southeast Asia – not far from the meadows where Mo Taylor and I first discovered hashish growing wild and paid some locals, who had no idea of its street value in Bangkok and Tokyo, to harvest it for us – I gave the performance of my life.

The hut was a little way beyond the edge of a village. As McDermott led me inside, I noticed a pen adjoining the hut, in which half-a-dozen pigs dipped their snouts into the muck and chomped at a long, red, tattered thing. I guessed what he was up to . . . McDermott, formerly of Belfast, formerly of the Ulster Volunteer Force, formerly of the human race.

The hut contained just two small windows in its wall facing the forest, so the interior was dim. A putrid smell tainted the air and there was a sound of buzzing flies that was almost machine-like. The flies swarmed over something on the hut's main item of furniture, a table about eight feet long in the middle of the floor.

I wanted to scream in pain and despair. I also felt close to ejecting the contents of my stomach. But I had to perform. In an offhand voice, I inquired, "Pigs?"

"Aye," said McDermott. "They leave nothing. Well, almost nothing. I mind years back there was a farmer in Country Tyrone who kept pigs, a squad of them, and one morning when he was in their pen filling the troughs he must have keeled over with a heart attack. By the time his family noticed him missing and went looking for him . . . There wasn't much left. Some hair. Bits of bone. His dentures. Of course, that involved a fierce number of pigs. Not the handful we have here. Though if you're willing to invest in a few *more* pigs . . . " He gestured towards the two village men who stood, watchful and silent, by the far wall. " . . . the community here would appreciate it."

I stared at him stony-faced. Generosity was not part of the image I projected just then.

He rambled on. "So, it'll take a wee while." He indicated the body on the table. Its left leg was missing, the upper thigh ending in a stump. "They're eating your man's leg just now. We've already fed them the soft parts, you know, the ones that go gassy and leaky and messy when they start getting ripe." He pointed to the torso. The body was naked and a long, wide gash ran from between the legs to the middle of the ribs, letting me see how everything underneath had been hollowed out. I noticed, too, what'd happened to the genitalia but, skilled actor that I was, didn't flinch. Then McDermott lifted the left arm by the wrist, showing me the reduced, mitten-shaped hand at the end of it. "And the fingers of course. His fingerprints are pig-shite now."

Still utterly impassive: "What about the teeth?"

They'd been removed. The lower part of his face, including the bottom of his nose and his whole chin, had gone. It'd been beaten down, leaving a grotesque hole that seemed to sink into his head and throat. McDermott removed a little cloth bag from a hook on one of the hut's columns. Things rattled inside. "I'll smash them up. Grind them as best I can. Then scatter them about the forest here. We'd have to be seriously unlucky if a trekker found a piece of one and identified it as being from a tooth."

Flies crawled in and out of the hole where the mouth had been, like they were mobbing the rim of an open jam-jar. Not a single facial muscle of mine twitched, giving away the repulsion I felt at the spectacle on the table, at McDermott, at myself for ordering this. "How long will it take? I can smell him already. The ordinary villagers will notice the stench if he's here much longer."

"Don't worry. There's a disused well out in the trees there. After dark, the boys will wrap him in plastic sheeting, sneak him over to that and put him inside. The water's cool, enough for him to stay fresh. Well, fresh-*ish*. And we'll keep retrieving him, and feeding a little more of him to the piggies each time, till he's all gone."

I gave McDermott a wad of notes, payment for a new electrical generator in the village headman's house – the local men present were two of his sons. I knew McDermott was impressed. I knew he'd soon be blabbing his big Northern Irish mouth about me. To his associates in the drugs trade, to people whom it was worth my while knowing.

"Aye, he had us chop up his pal, his partner. And he was cool as a fucking cucumber about it!"

I stepped out of the hut, knowing that halfway down the road from here I would have to stop the pickup and vomit, lengthily and savagely, into the roadside foliage. But hey . . . What acting I'd done then. Worthy of an Oscar.

Bravo!

***

I'd locked all 25 known drawers. And yet, that night, I dreamt I went into the study, reached for one of them, and had no difficulty sliding it out. The same beam of internal light, the same smell of citrus and jasmine. This time, the drawer was obscenely packed with tangled, glistening intestines.

And afterwards, when I awoke in my bed, *she* was there. For a moment. Glowering at me with her red eyes, grimacing foully, weeping . . . Before she disappeared.

I found the real drawer in the real study open, as I'd left it in the dream. The only difference was that its key had been placed in and jutted from its keyhole.

FIVE

Mr. Lim spent his days in a shopping centre along the road from the condo-building crowned by our penthouse. The centre had been built in the 1970s and feted then as one of the first air-conditioned places of its kind in Singapore. But nowadays it looked shabby. By modern standards its retailing spaces were small and cramped, occupied by modest hairdressing, nail and skincare salons, stationery shops, private tuition schools, and agencies for hiring maids and nannies. There was more diversity, though, in a sunken alleyway that ran in front of the centre's basement, a dozen feet below street level. The businesses lining the alleyway included bars and eateries, a tailor, a florist, and Mr. Lim's antiques shop.

It was six o'clock when I descended from the street into the alleyway. The day had begun to lose its heat and brightness. His antiques shop remained open, but he sat on a chair outside, next to a little table with an opened bottle of wine and two half-full wine glasses. Seated on the table's other side was a woman in her early sixties. Her age hadn't deterred her from sporting a headful of bright, yellow-dyed hair, or wearing a tight pair of jeans and a T-shirt bearing the face of some recent K-pop idol. I assumed this was the proprietress of the salon next door to Mr. Lim's shop.

"Can I speak to you?" I nodded respectfully to the woman. "When you're free?"

For the first time, I saw Mr. Lim smile. Probably the wine was an early-evening ritual that helped him unwind. "Well," he said, "I'm discussing business with Mrs. Kheong here." He gestured along the alleyway to an area of tables and benches outside a pub entrance. "But perhaps I could join you after ten minutes? I drink only wine, but friends of mine recommend that place for its selection of craft beers."

I ordered a beer and sat at a table. The tiles covering the alleyway's floor were scuffed and cracked, the air smelt faintly of drains, and trellises supporting plastic vines and flowers had been set against the streetside wall to hide its stained and blistered paintwork. Yet the pub attracted a good-sized crowd that included Singaporean hipsters and well-to-do foreigners. I tried not to eavesdrop on the surrounding conversations, but soon found myself doing so. In particular, I listened to two young English guys – backpackers, no doubt. I suspected their high spirits were due to the fact that they'd just arrived, found a place to stay, and dropped off their packs there. Unencumbered, they could relax and enjoy the city for a while.

Exploring the world during their youth . . . While it still seemed a vast, new place, teeming with things to discover, with opportunities . . . I thought of Mo Taylor and myself a long time before –

"Mr. Grant?" The antiques dealer settled onto the bench facing me, then showed a look of concern. "Are you all right?"

The table was equipped with a packet of napkins and I used one to wipe away my tears. "It's nothing," I said. "It's sunscreen. I put on sunscreen before I came out, then started sweating, and the sweat made it run into my eyes."

He seemed unconvinced, but his tone became business-like. "What can I do for you this time?"

"It's connected with what you did for me *last* time. And it's strange, I'm afraid."

I took care not to say too much. I didn't describe my dreams about the contents of the drawers or mention the ghoulish figure that kept appearing after I woke up. I merely said that since the drawers' arrival, I'd been plagued by nightmares and my home generally had acquired a bad vibe.

Not unexpectedly, Mr. Lim looked bemused. But at least he sounded like he took me seriously. "This is outside my field of expertise, Mr. Grant. But I'll introduce you to people who *might* help you."

When I'd finished my beer, he led me towards an end of the alleyway I hadn't been in before. We passed a calligraphy school, a shop selling tropical fish, a grocery store with racks of packaged food parked outside it, a *dojo* where waiting mothers watched their white-clad kids performing martial-arts moves through the windows. We stopped at a façade with a bright orange sign above its door.

I said, "I don't believe it. Not in this city."

"Search beneath Singapore's shiny, modern surface," said Mr. Lim mysteriously, "and you'll be surprised at what quaint, old things you find."

I read the name on the sign: "Ghost Catchers."

SIX

The girl held up her phone. "Do you mind if I record you?"

I tensed. Survival instincts that'd been baked into my system years ago warned me it was *not* safe to have my voice and image recorded. God knows where they might end up and who might hear or see them . . . But I made myself relax. I told myself the situations that'd forged those instincts were history now. And then I gave her a full version of events – not the edited one I'd given Mr. Lim. The only part I avoided was how the things I'd dreamt were in the drawers could be linked with my past.

Afterwards, she used her phone's camera to take photos of the chest of drawers from different angles. She also had me open the drawers that I remembered opening in the dreams and took shots of their interiors, though she didn't say if she detected the psychic residues of phantom teeth, fingers, intestines, or legs –

Oh yes. The previous night, after Mr. Lim had introduced me to the Ghost Catchers shop, I'd had another dream. This time the drawer I'd pulled open contained a badly-gnawed piece of leg. And when I woke in my bedroom, she was there on cue, simultaneously weeping in anguish and leering in malevolence.

The girl took a laptop from her bag. Her only equipment appeared to be that, her phone, and a tiny thermometer she'd placed on top of the chest of drawers. I'd expected her to bring special cameras and camcorders with infra-red night vision, and motion detectors, and gadgets for measuring electromagnetic fields, so to me she seemed low-budget and amateurish.

Despite it being called Ghost Catchers, I'd got the impression that the shop's primary business wasn't hunting ghosts. Rather, most customers came for fortune telling – "destiny consultations" – or advice on *fengshui*. I wondered if this kooky girl had fancied herself as a paranormal investigator and pestered Ghost Catchers until they gave her a job or, at least, an internship. Maybe now they sent her to deal with their more unhinged-sounding customers. Ones like myself.

I studied her while she placed her laptop on the floor, knelt and started typing on it. She had bobbed hair and wore glasses, a green T-shirt, flared jeans and suede boots. She resembled a compendium of characters from *Scooby Doo* – Velma's head, Shaggy's torso, Fred's legs and feet.

Typing, she mused, "You know, your description of this ghost sounds like a *Pontianak*."

"Pontianak? That's a city in Borneo."

"Yes, but *Pontianak* is also the name of a creature in Indonesian, Malaysian, and Singaporean folklore. She has the features you mentioned. Red eyes, long black hair, white skin, sharp fingernails, a white dress . . . And she's crying when you see her?"

"Yes."

"Supposedly, sobbing sounds tell you when a *Pontianak* is close. Some say she takes the form of a pregnant woman. Pregnant, but never able to give birth – maybe that's why she sobs. Also, you say when you open the drawers in the dreams, there's a smell?"

"Yes. Like jasmine . . . and citrus . . ."

"Frangipani. The smell of that flower accompanies her, supposedly." On the laptop she tapped some words into Google and a half-minute later had something to show me. "Here. Even in Singapore today, people claim to have seen one. To have actually filmed one."

On her screen I watched some footage, shot on a phone presumably, of a traffic roundabout at night-time. The road encircled an area of grass that had four mature rain-trees rising up from it. Under one of the trees' canopies, among the mesh of its lower branches, something pale fluttered.

"*Pontianak* like trees. They choose one as their base, to lurk in or under. Though usually not this type of tree. Usually it's a banana tree – "

I interrupted. "A banana tree isn't really a tree. It's a giant herb." I gave the screen a contemptuous wave. "And that isn't a *Pontianak*. It isn't even a figure. It's just a bedsheet that blew off someone's washing line and got caught in those branches."

Ignoring my scepticism, the girl got up and turned towards the chest of drawers again. "I wonder if that contains wood from a tree associated with a *Pontianak*?"

"You think these drawers brought a local ghost into my home?"

"Not a ghost, Mr. Grant. The *Pontianak* is a vampire."

"What?"

"Probably that's the closest creature in Western folklore. Though according to some legends, the *Pontianak* doesn't only feed on blood. She uses her fingernails to tear out a victim's organs and eat those. Or suck his eyes out of his head."

"His? The victims are men?"

"So the legends say."

"I'm sorry. You might be able, just, to persuade me that ghosts exist. But I draw the line at believing in vampires."

She lifted her laptop and returned it to her bag. "You never met a vampire before?"

"No. Have you?"

"Possibly . . . You could say my ex-boyfriend was a vampire. He drank away my life-force. After him, I felt so weak I thought I would die. He didn't drink my blood, of course. He drank all my hope, my self-respect. He built up my expectations, then smashed them down again. He broke promises. He flattered me, then attacked me with horrible insults. He gaslighted me . . . And as I suffered, he seemed to grow stronger. Maybe he was a psychic vampire. A vampire of the emotions." Shuddering, she slung her bag over her shoulder. "Anyway. I'll go back and give this information to Grand Master Koay."

I was still processing what she'd said about vampires. *Grand Master Koay?* I thought vaguely. *Related to Grand Master Flash?* "Then what happens?"

"He'll decide what to do. Perhaps he'll suggest an exorcism . . . Meanwhile, tell us if anything else occurs."

I escorted her to the lift while messaging my man downstairs that the guest was leaving. I employed several guards, on constant rotation, with one always on duty at the lift's bottom. It was something I'd agreed to with the building's management. My guards wore the same uniforms as the place's normal security staff, to blend in, but their sole duty was monitoring people trying to access our penthouse. Ensuring anyone I didn't want up here didn't get up here. The lift was already in motion. I was surprised when its doors opened and revealed my wife and two of the maids, laden with bags of shopping. I hadn't expected her to return so soon.

Once the lift-doors had shut on the girl from Ghost Catchers, and the maids had lugged the shopping to one of the bedrooms, she demanded, "Who was that?"

Time to play-act again, to lie. "She's one of Mr. Lim's staff. I noticed a flaw in the chest of drawers and wanted someone to look at it. The front of it has a slight discolouration. Mr. Lim missed that somehow when he purchased it for me."

"I didn't see anything wrong."

"I spotted it just the other evening. It's visible only in a certain light."

Mie didn't seem convinced by the explanation, so I braced myself for further questions. But then her suspicious expression softened. A trace of concern appeared on her features. "Is there something the matter with you?"

"What makes you think that?"

"Your eyes look red. Wet . . . "

"I think I'm suffering from an allergy."

"In Singapore?"

"Well, they love boasting about how many trees they've planted on their little island. Seven million, is it? Look out of the window. It's as much a green jungle as a concrete one. The air must be thick with pollen."

Thankfully, I didn't have to lie any more in that direction, either, for then one of the maids returned and asked her where she wanted some of her new clothes hung. She bustled off in her white dress that almost disguised the bulge of her belly. I really didn't appreciate that white dress today. Nor how she'd let her long, black hair hang loose.

SEVEN

Later, I realised I'd forgotten to ask the would-be paranormal investigator an important question and texted her on the burner-phone I was using for this matter. I'd already let her record me, and there was nothing criminal about being haunted, but nonetheless I didn't want my dealings with Ghost Catchers traceable on one of my official phones.

I asked: "How do you kill this creature? Put a stake through her heart?"

I'd meant the last words as a joke but in her reply she took them seriously. "No. Not a stake and not the heart. To stop a *Pontianak*, you stick a nail into the base of her neck."

Our top-of-the-range penthouse was equipped with top-of-the-range repair and maintenance toolkits. I entered its storeroom, a square, windowless room with a hulking, metal door that also acted as its bomb shelter, a feature of every Singaporean house and apartment built since the Civil Defence Shelter Act was passed in 1997. There, I searched through several plastic cases whose moulded interiors seemed to hold every tool and tool-accessory imaginable. Eventually, I found a round-headed steel nail about 15 centimetres long.

It was nonsense, of course. But if my career in crime had taught me anything, it was best to take no chances. To be prepared for all eventualities, no matter how unlikely or illogical they appeared.

Just then the phone beeped with another message. The girl had more information. "According to some stories, a nail in the neck doesn't kill a *Pontianak*. It turns her into a beautiful, demure and obedient woman. She stays like that unless the nail is pulled out again."

***

When I returned to the study, the natural light had faded outside and the artificial glow of the nocturnal city had replaced it.

I saw the blemish again. It was a pale spot on the second drawer down in the right-end column. I tried to remember when I'd first noticed it. In reality or during one of the dreams? Approaching it, I realised it was really beneath the drawer, and it extended to the top of the next drawer down. Around the spot fanned the branches of one of the carved trees. I wondered what it reminded me of, then shivered when I recalled the white shape hovering amid the tree-branches in that alleged footage of a *Pontianak*.

As before, the blemish faded when I came close, but I'd memorised its position on the narrow strip of wood between the two drawers. I crouched and probed the area with a fingertip and felt a faint roughness on its surface. The more I explored it, the more convinced I became there was a hole in the wood, hardly a centimetre high, just millimetres across, which'd been filled with some other material.

I carried the nail from the storeroom. I used its tip to gouge at the spot. Crumbs of stuff – not wood – fell out.

I finally unplugged another keyhole that'd been concealed between the two drawers. A 26th one. For the first time, I picked up the 26th key from the very end of Mr. Lim's cloth. Presumably, it had the letter Z moulded and imprinted on its bit. I crouched again and inserted the key in the new hole. It fitted and turned.

After much fumbling, I managed to ease out of the strip separating the two drawers a much smaller and thinner drawer. It had the dimensions of a slim paperback book and its interior was capable of holding nothing thicker than a few sheets of paper.

And that was what it contained – a sheet of yellowed parchment with a handwritten script on it.

I went to the glass wall, where there was just enough light coming in for me to discern the script. The language baffled me. It certainly wasn't Arabic or Chinese or the indigenous Japanese alphabets of hiragana or katakana. It lacked the loops and arches of Thai, the sharper twists and turns of Tamil, the bubble-like appearance of Sinhala, the precise lines of Korean hangul, the hanging-from-a-pole look of Devanagari. This mysterious language seemed older than all of them.

Mr. Lim had said there were no receipts for the purchase of the chest of drawers among the merchant's papers. So, had he received it as a gift? A secretly malicious gift, from someone privately harbouring a grudge against him? Someone who hated him so much that they hid among the drawers a spell, a curse, an invocation summoning a hideous *Pontianak*?

I recalled the girl's remarks about vampires, about them not necessarily feeding on blood, about some of them feeding on emotions, too. The merchant had been a reclusive man. What did he have to hide? What had been his secrets? If he'd been anything like me, I could imagine those secrets.

Perhaps this particular *Pontianak* fed on . . . guilt.

Then, standing at the glass wall, I had a sensation of not being alone. Though the door hadn't creaked, someone had entered the study and was behind me, watching. I should turn, obviously, and see who that person was. But suddenly my skin prickled, my stomach felt nauseous, my breath was tense and tight. I really didn't want to turn around.

After an interminable length of time, I did hear a sound behind me. A drawer scraped as it was slowly pulled open.

Much more time passed before I managed to turn. I saw no figure. The room was as empty as it'd been when I entered. I returned to the chest of drawers and wasn't surprised when I detected the smell of frangipani and saw light rising from the opened drawer. Bracing myself, I peered into it . . .

I experienced the greatest jolt of horror yet. This time, however, instead of waking – for surely I was in another nightmare – I was flung back in time.

I had a flashback to the innocent era when we'd been travellers, not aspiring entrepreneurs in the drugs trade. We were staying in a hostel in Chiang Mai in northern Thailand. One afternoon, in the communal bathroom, I stripped off and entered the shower area. A row of showerheads sprouted from its wall and I discovered Mo standing under the furthest-away one, about to turn on its tap. For a moment we stood awkwardly, butt-naked, staring at one another . . . Then he approached me, reached to the wrist of my right hand, and steered the hand down to his penis, which was already swollen and stiff.

I could hardly protest. Mine was the same way.

While he raised his other hand and began caressing my face, I tried to resist what was happening. Most of me didn't want to resist it, but I heard a voice belonging to a harder, more calculating part of my personality. It warned me this was not a good idea. I was making myself vulnerable . . . Vulnerable to what, I didn't know. Perhaps to some danger that awaited me in the future.

So he touched me, and I touched him, and all I could say in resistance was: "You know I like girls as well."

He smiled. "Well, lucky you. Getting the best of both worlds."

Poor Mo. As it turned out, I wanted the best of all worlds. That included a world where I could live without mistrust and paranoia, which had tragic consequences for him.

I was back in the study, looking down at what lay inside the drawer. By itself, exuding a few strings of skin and tissue where McDermott's blade had severed it, it seemed so tiny and pathetic. So shrivelled and flattened, so pitifully different from what I'd touched that afternoon in the showers . . .

I started screaming.

***

My screams continued after the nightmare ended and I lay thrashing amid my bedclothes. And then, as I fell silent and became still on the bed, I realised more bad things were to come. She would appear soon.

Instinctively, my hand scooted out to the bedside table, where it found the iron nail. This rested on a sheet of paper that felt dry and parchment-like . . . I was confused. Hadn't my discovery of the invocation in the 26th drawer happened in the dream? How could it be here with me, in reality?

Suddenly, on cue again, she loomed over me while I was still on the bed. Black, serpentine tresses of hair coiled about her face. A long, white dress streamed from her shoulders . . .

I sprang up from the bed and managed to get an arm around her head before I fell back. Dragging her down with me, I plunged the nail into her nape. A liquid warmth spurted over my fingers. Her limbs flailed and muffled cries came from where her face was crushed against my chest. Moments later, the movements and sounds ceased and she slumped over me. I let go and tried to shift from under her. As I did this, she rolled over the edge of the bed and landed on the floor.

The door opened and the light came on . . . No, the door was already open and a shaft of light was already slanting in from the main corridor. A maid who was on night-duty and staying in the bedroom next to my wife's one – the other staff, when off-duty, resided in two apartments below ours – had arrived in the open doorway and flicked the light-switch. Now the whole bedroom was bright.

The maid screamed at what she saw. I clawed my way to bed's edge and looked down at the figure lying on the floor. Blood crept out from under her neck and began to stain the adjacent, fanned-out strands of hair. I perceived her face and understood that what the girl had said was true.

Once a nail was planted in the base of her neck, a *Pontianak* changed. She was no longer a monster but a beautiful and demure woman.

EIGHT

After inspecting the front of the chest of drawers, and admiring the four carved trees with their intricate patterns of branches, my father-in-law rose to his feet. An arthritic click came from his knees. "It's beautiful," he said. "How did you find it?"

I knew the old man valued modesty and hated big-headedness, so I admitted, "I had help. I commissioned a man called Lim, a local antiques dealer. I'll arrange for you to meet him sometime. I'm sure the two of you will have much to talk about."

He produced a smile – for him, the rarest of things. "This is a wonderful gift, Alan. I'm grateful."

I smiled too. My wife stood beside me and I slipped an arm around her waist. Our son slept against her breasts, cocooned in the cotton folds of a baby carrier-wrap. "I'm simply glad it pleases you . . . "

My voice trailed away. The arm with which I was holding Mei felt damp. I looked behind her and discovered a great, red stain spreading down the back of her white dress. The redness seemed to leak out from under the tresses of her hair and the ones covering the back of her neck were wet and matted. I grabbed a handful of that hair and yanked it up.

Just above her dress's back neckline, the head of a nail protruded an inch from her neck. Without thinking, I put my fingers around the nail-head and pulled its iron shaft out of her flesh. The shaft made a soft, sucking noise as it emerged. More blood spouted from the hole it left behind.

Mei dropped to the floor, the baby still huddled against her. I stood over them, holding the nail in my bloodied fingers. *Caught red-handed*, I thought stupidly.

Distantly, I heard her father cry, "What have you *done* to her?"

***

I was too accustomed to these nightmares to wake from them struggling and screaming anymore. All I felt was a grim resignation. I slowly sat up and swung my legs over the edge of the bed. Despite its narrowness, the bed took up most of the space in the prison cell. Tonight, the brickwork in the cell's walls had a strange, brownish hue, so that it resembled the inside of a giant drawer. One that'd been fashioned out of teakwood.

I cradled my face in my hands but didn't weep. I couldn't. It was as if something had drained all the grief from me.

Yet she remained – perhaps hoping there were a last few morsels of guilt, sorrow and pain I could provide her with. Now she crouched along the bed by me. Her eyes glowered redly, her mouth made its rictus and bared its twisted teeth, her cheeks glistened with soulless tears.

Sitting there together, we must have looked a grotesque but appropriate couple. Practically husband and wife.

Where the Stars Don't Shine

Robert Allen Lupton

Captain Jefferson Redfeather sat up in the Longsleep chamber, rubbed his eyes, and promptly vomited into his own lap. The bright liquid crystal diode lights hurt his eyes. Things didn't feel right. He was alone. There should have been technicians, human and robotic, welcoming him back to wakefulness.

He checked the perpetual clock on the chamber's readout panel. Six-hundred-eighty-four years, two months, nine days, and a few hours. He knew something was wrong. Travel time to Sirius was nine hundred years. He shouldn't be awake.

He unplugged the nutrient feed from his left arm and the blood drip from his right. Food came through one arm and blood to be cleaned and replaced flowed in and out of the other. He was dizzy and disorientated. He felt badly dehydrated. That shouldn't be. Maybe his nutrient feed malfunctioned and his chamber defaulted into wakeup mode.

He drank a container of vitamin water and vomited again.

He looked around the sleep chamber for the ship's officers and crew. The chamber was separate from the massive rooms where over five-hundred-thousand colonists were cryogenically frozen for the voyage. The crew and officers traveled in a state of suspended animation rather than as peoplesickles, like paying passengers.

He verbally logged on to the computer. "Athena, Redfeather here, authorization code LR212108. Status report, please. Why am I awake?"

"Good morning, Captain. I trust you slept well. This is ship's day 249,901. Life support is fully functional and we are on schedule and on course. Almost fifty thousand of the cryogenic chambers have ceased to function or are offline."

"Have the pilots investigated?"

"I have had no communication with either pilot in 195,361 days."

"No communication? Why didn't you wake me sooner?"

"Protocol. The ship is on schedule and on course. Lack of communication is not a sleep termination triggering event. Seven hours ago, cryogenic chamber TB2705 went offline. Its failure triggered the ten-percent failure threshold that requires me to wake the captain. I have complied."

"Where are the pilots?"

"As you know, the pilots do not appear on my monitors. I cannot detect their locations."

"What about the status chips embedded in their necks?"

"The chips haven't moved in 195,361 days. The chips are in the control room, but surveillance indicates that the control room has been unoccupied for 195,361 days."

"Thank you, Athena. Wake First Officer, Kendara Kamaguchi, and Security Officer, Greg Flynn. We'll conduct a physical investigation of the control room and the colonist storage halls."

The soft hum of machinery filled the room and bright lighting filled two of the sleeping cylinders. Redfeather checked the readouts. It would be over an hour before the process was completed. Kendara was as beautiful as ever. It would be nice to talk to his First Officer and fiancée again. After all, it had been over six hundred years.

His stomach rumbled. He decided to spend the hour in the officer's mess eating his first meal in over half a millennium and reviewing the ship's log. The door slid open behind him. He thought that must be one of the pilots. He turned and what appeared to be the bushy tail of a black dog was briefly visible before the door closed.

A dog's tail. The closest thing to live animals on board were the frozen fertilized eggs stored in the supply hold. Dogs, cats, sheep, cattle, chickens, and a hundred other species waited to be born on Sirius Four. The crew joked that this ship was going to the dogs. Redfeather closed his eyes and took several deep breaths. He whispered to himself. "There's no dog. Hallucinations. You've been asleep for over six centuries. A little food and a little time for your brain synapses to wake up and you'll be fine."

He reflected briefly on the vision quests that were a rite of passage for young men of his ancestral Apache heritage. Those men walked into the desert and fasted until they found their spirit animal, who would guide them their entire lives. They fasted for six or seven days before they saw visions. He'd fasted for almost seven hundred years. He spoke to the waking Kamaguchi, "Sweetheart, I should be happy I saw a dog. I'd hate for my spirit animal to be a chicken or a goat."

He stepped over the small black hairs in the hallway outside the door without noticing them. He ordered a protein drink in the galley and spoke to the computer screen embedded in the table. "Athena, scroll the log. I'll stop you if I want to review anything. Let me know just before Kendara and Greg wake up. I want to be there."

"Scrolling log."

Redfeather watched the days and years roll by. After two hundred years of uneventful entries, he said, "Athena, just show me any unusual entries. Focus on the pilots."

All pilots received a treatment developed during the early stages of the diaspora to the stars by Eastern European scientists. At first, the process was immediately fatal to over ninety percent of recipients, but eventually trial and error demonstrated that people of Slavic descent responded better than the general population. Bartok and Nadia received the treatment four days before departure. They both transitioned successfully and about the time the ship passed the orbit of Neptune, they were strapped in place and hooked up to their IVs. Redfeather remembered turning control over to the pair from Budapest. "See you in a thousand years, more or less."

"Da, Captain. Sleep well. Nadia and I will watch over you like the fairy godmothers, yes."

The log showed that Boris and Nadia never slept and never left their posts. They received intravenous nourishment on schedule until 195,311 days ago when the log showed a significant decrease in the pilots' nutrient solution. The level of nutrients grew less daily and dropped to zero the day before the pilots vanished.

Too bad, thought Redfeather. They were nice kids. He believed the whole idea of live pilots was foolish. Athena was capable of handling anything that could be dealt with during an interstellar voyage, but humanity has an almost pathological mistrust of machines and people insisted on having humans in charge. Nine hundred years is a long time and if the Methuselah Protocol hadn't been developed, who knows how the millennium-long flights could have been managed.

He wasn't looking forward to visiting the command center. He expected to find the pilots' decayed bodies. Starvation was one hell of a way to die.

"Captain, First Officer Kendara Kamaguchi is almost awake. Her brain activity shows she is having a nightmare. She could injure herself."

Redfeather ran to the sleep chamber thankful for the artificial gravity Athena maintained at all times during the trip. Once she established the spin, it took no energy to maintain it in space.

He didn't notice the wiry black hairs stuck to the bottom of his right foot.

The lid to Kendara's chamber slid open. She sat up and screamed. He held her, but she pounded his chest with her fists. Then she vomited. After a moment she said, "Bats. I woke up and bats were scratching the lid of my chamber. They bit at the plasteel. I was terrified."

"Just a nightmare. I imagined I saw a big dog when I woke up. It will pass. Greg will wake up soon. The pilots are offline. I'm sure they're dead. Let's verify everything else on board is okay and go back to sleep. We still have a hundred years to go."

Kendara rinsed her mouth and smiled. "Are you Sirius?"

Redfeather laughed. "Yes, I am. You must be feeling better."

A warning light flashed on Greg's chamber and the lid slid open. The three officers showered, dressed in clean clothes, and reluctantly went to the Command Center. Greg Flynn said, "Maybe the Methuselah Protocol didn't work properly for Greg and Nadia. I never trusted it anyway. People can't stay awake and alive for a thousand years. We've sent hundreds of ships to the stars with Methuselah pilots on board, but they're one-way trips. We don't know if it works. Hell, we don't even know if a single ship even reached its destination."

Redfeather said, "True, but that doesn't change our duty."

The pilot's command chairs in Control Central were empty. The feeding and waste removal tubes were neatly coiled on the seats and two status chips sat side by side on the console between the two seats. The room was not in disarray. The helmets, microphones, and interactive reality gloves had been stowed like Bartok and Nadia left for a few minutes to take a shower, have a beer, or perform a visual inspection of the ship.

Kendara picked up the two status chips. "Except for this, I'd say that our pilots will be back any moment, ignoring the fact that Athena reports that our pilots removed these chips a few hundred years ago. Even with the Methuselah treatment, they have to eat and drink. Once they detached themselves from their feeding tubes, their days were numbered."

Redfeather ran his hands along a feeding tube. "This was removed intentionally. The needle isn't damaged. Perhaps the centuries were too long. I expect I'd lose my mind if I were facing hundreds of years strapped in this chair. They may have decided to unhook themselves and live out the best life they could make for themselves on this ship."

Greg spoke to Athena. "Did the pilots access food supplies? Where was the last place you saw them?"

"Food supplies were untouched and I last detected them in this room. Bartok removed his chip and disappeared from my monitors. Nadia vanished eighty-four seconds later."

"I don't understand."

"One side-effect of the Methuselah injections is that recipients are not visible to a ship's monitors or cameras. I can't see them."

Greg shook his head. "That's ridiculous. There are other ways. Their body temperature will raise the temperature of whatever room they're in. Not only that, if they move anything or open a door, it would show up on your monitors."

"Agreed. The door to CH3, Cryogenic Hall Three, opened once and closed 195,359 days ago. All visual and auditory monitors inside that hall are non-functional. I can monitor the status of the individual chambers. That's why I woke you. One chamber goes offline every day."

Redfeather said, "Alright, I want to inspect CH3. Show us the way."

"Follow the yellow flashing lights."

The door slid open and the officers stepped inside. The gigantic room was a charnel house. Hundreds, no thousands, of the cryogenic chambers were open and empty. Bodies, headless bodies, littered the floor. The corpses seemed mummified and the dry flesh was tautly stretched and the faces of the severed heads were drawn into horrid smiles and grimaces. A thin haze drifted aimlessly through the room. It stank of old garbage and spoiled milk.

Greg vomited at the sweet stench. "My sweet lord, what hell is this?"

Redfeather paused and turned on his shoulder camera. "I don't have a clue. It can't be a malfunction of some sort. Athena, can you see this through my camera."

"I have visual and audio. Please walk closer."

"I think not," said Redfeather. "Athena, wake the rest of the crew. Close this door behind us. Do not open it again without my express orders. Acknowledge, please."

"Acknowledged, Captain. Reanimation of crew personnel commenced."

"I want full access to the pilots' files and the weapons room."

"Their files are loaded to your personal data stream and the weapons room door is activated and keyed to your retinal scan."

Redfeather and Kendara helped Greg from the room. Redfeather said, "I want to be there when the rest of the crew wakes up."

The door closed, but an insubstantial, barely visible mist drifted into the hallway. Kendara held her nose. "What the hell? The stinking miasma followed us out of the room. Athena, are there microbes or viruses in this smoke."

"I do not detect any smoke. Perhaps, you should point the camera directly at it."

"I am. It's right here."

The smoke or haze or mist swirled and two indistinct faces appeared briefly and vanished with the fog into the air ducts along the floor of the hallway. Kendara gasped, "Faces. I saw faces in the smoke."

Athena said, "My monitors are clear."

"Faces in the Mist. Sounds like a bad horror novel. Let's get moving," said Redfeather. "The air scrubbers will clean whatever mist made it out of CH3. Don't worry about it."

"I saw what I saw. If the air scrubbers are functioning properly, why was the air hazy in the CH3? Athena?"

"There is no haze in Cryogenic Hall Three."

The captain said, "Let it go, Kendara. With all those dead bodies, the air has to be a little foul. The scrubbers aren't designed to handle that kind of load."

Greg said, "I think we should run a diagnostic on Athena. She says there's no smoke, but we all saw it. She says she can't see the pilots. I'm sure they're long dead, but Athena should see their bodies."

Redfeather agreed. "Athena, full diagnostic please."

"Running self-diagnostic."

Redfeather, Kendara, and Greg helped the other six crew personnel complete the reanimation process. Marda was very weak. Greg propped her up and gave her water. "Somehow, her feeding tube became restricted. Her nutrient supply was reduced by less than a hundredth of a percent, but that's enough to slowly starve her over the years. She needs medical care until she regains her strength."

Redfeather checked Marda's vitals himself. "She barely weighs a hundred pounds. Take her to sickbay."

Greg and Leo, the newly awakened medic, carried her from the room. Leo said, "I'll get her on another intravenous feed right away and get a fluid and vitamin drip started. I'll do a full workup and design a custom nutrient solution for her."

Redfeather waited until Greg and Leo returned to explain the situation to the crew. Carl, Anna, Susanne, and Hiroshi used the time to wash and dress. Carl poured a cup of coffee, smelled the aroma, and smiled. "Can I pour anyone else a cup?"

Greg and Leo returned from sickbay. Greg said, "Thanks, I'd love one. We sedated Marda. She'll need a few weeks to regain her strength. Has Athena finished her diagnostic? Sickbay smelled funny. There's got to be some kind of malfunction in the air supply."

Leo took a sip of a blended green concoction and wiped the lime-colored foam from his upper lip. "I was uncomfortable in sickbay. It felt like someone was watching me."

Kendara laughed, "Twilight Zone. Athena's always watching. She knows if you've been good or bad."

"No, not like that," said Leo. "It was like someone else was in the room."

Greg said, 'I didn't feel anything like that, but there was a slight haze. That's why I think we need to do a complete analysis of the air supply system."

Redfeather said, "Agreed. Athena, display air supply status."

"Certainly, the data is on the wall monitor. The air supply system is operating within acceptable parameters. I have completed my self-diagnostic and I am operating perfectly."

"Jefferson, I think we should visually confirm the air supply status," said Kendara.

"Agreed, my dear. Carl and Greg, that's yours to do. Go though it in detail. The rest of us will clean the mess in CH3. Everything goes into the organic recycler. This is a bad job, but we've got it to do. Containment suits and individual air supply for everyone. The sooner we're done, the sooner we can go back to sleep."

Leo washed his glass. "And the pilots?"

"They may be two of the bodies. Verify DNA on every single corpse before recycling. If Bartok and Nadia aren't dead in CH3, we'll need to search the entire ship. Enough talk, let's suit up and get to work."

***

Kendara's eyes burned. She wanted to rub them, but she couldn't reach inside her containment suit. She tried to scratch her forehead against the inside of her helmet. This was dirty nasty work. Fifty-thousand bodies for nine people to identify and clean up. That came to almost five-thousand bodies for each crew member. They'd activated and programmed equipment to do the heavy lifting and decontamination, but each body had to be identified and logged before it was loaded on a lorry and taken to recycling. She'd fallen into a numbed routine by the third morning. One ID a minute, sixty per hour, and ten-hour shifts, do the math. Six-hundred corpses processed per person per shift worked out to over 90 total shifts, or ten shifts each.

At first, the carnage disgusted and frightened Kendara. By her third shift, bodies torn asunder, throats ripped out, and entrails strewn across the room lost their individuality. The dead ceased to become people in her mind, but only a job to be finished. She couldn't handle it any other way and remain sane. She ignored the agonized faces, the limbs laying akimbo, and the decayed flesh dried to the consistency of beef jerky.

Hiroshi sat on the floor to her right with his head in his lap. Kendara read the identification of the body she had just sampled, "Mark Robertson." Mark and his wife, Patricia, were veterinarians from Corn Valley, Iowa. She stopped reading about the dead man and patted Hiroshi.

He flinched when she touched his shoulder. "You okay?" she asked.

This girl is from my hometown. I knew her. She was my sister's age. I can't do this anymore. I'm afraid the rest of her family may be here."

"I'll finish up this area. Our shifts are over in forty minutes. Take off now, get cleaned up, and fix a meal for everyone. I'll stay longer and make up your lost time."

Hiroshi slipped and almost fell when he stood. Kendara checked the next body and Hiroshi was right, the corpse was a fifty percent match to the girl from Hiroshi's hometown. It was her sister.

Kendara finished her shift and changed clothes before joining the others for dinner. Hiroshi put a plate of beef noodles in front of her. He silently mouthed, "Thank you."

Athena spoke before Kendara answered. "Marda is no longer connected to my monitors. Her readings have terminated."

Jefferson Redfeather yelled, "Athena, is she dead?"

"Undetermined. She is no longer connected . . . "

Redfeather was out the door before she completed her sentence. He ran. The door to sickbay was open. Marda's body, tangled in sheets and sensors, dangled head down from the bed. Her bloodless flesh was whiter than the sheets on her bed. Susanne lifted Marda by her ice-cold arms and shoved her onto the bed. Tears were in her eyes. She struggled to reconnect the tangled monitor cables and IV tubes.

Leo checked Marda's wrist for a pulse. He didn't find one and reached for her neck. A bloodless gash gaped open under her jaw. Leo gently took Susanne's hands. "Stop it. She's gone. Look at her throat."

Kendara backed against the wall. "Jefferson, maybe you did see a dog. I thought we were all together. Athena, what happened here?"

"I have video. It's on the wall monitor.

Marda was asleep and began to bounce and thrash around. Her monitors ripped loose and the IVs jumped from her arm. Blood welled from a gash in her throat only to vanish as quickly as it appeared. Marda slumped down and slid partially off the bed. Seconds later, Jefferson entered the room, Susanne shoved him aside and ran to Marda.

"That's enough, Athena. Do you have an explanation?"

"I do not."

"You can't see Bartok or Nadia, they could have done this."

"Possibly, but they do not appear on my screens. The most logical answer is that they are dead. In theory, they could be responsible."

"Athena, stop telling me the pilots don't appear on your screens. I know that. Run full scans of the body. I'd like Leo to perform a physical autopsy. Double shifts in CH3 tomorrow. I want that room clean and if the pilots' bodies are in that mess, I want them found. Athena, send Bartok's and Nadia's files to everyone to review and read. We'll talk in fourteen hours. I want details on the Methuselah system for me to review. Let's get to it, people. I don't want to sound heartless, but crying over Marda won't help her or us."

***

The next three shifts in the charnel house passed without incident. Anna closed the door to CH3 and reinforced the "Do Not Open" order with Athena. She removed her hood leaned against the wall, closed her eyes, and breathed deeply. She almost fell asleep, but a growl brought her to instant attention.

A large wolf bristled in front of her. Its teeth were bared and the fur on its shoulders stood on end. The click of sharp claws echoed in the corridor. A second wolf moved closer. Anna winked at the animals. Anna said, "Athena, don't respond verbally, patch me through to the rest of the crew. Redfeather, I'm in the corridor outside the cryogenic hall. Two large dogs, no, two wolves are about to attack me. I'll try to get into the hall and close the door behind me."

The wolves moved closer. They stank of old death. Clotted blood stained their muzzles and pieces of bone flecked their hair. Anna almost whispered. "Athena, on my count to three, open the door behind me. The second I'm clear, close it. Don't let the wolves inside."

Athena said, "You are alone in the corridor."

"Just do it, damn it. One. Two. Three."

Anna moved into the doorway and blocked it open with her body. After the wolves moved through the doorway, Anna shouted, "Athena, close the door."

The wolves' bodies became blurry and indistinct. They shifted into smoke that boiled and rolled. They assumed human forms. Anna hugged the female. "Nadia, my beloved ancestor. I was so worried. Why the hell are you wandering around the damn ship? You were supposed to pilot until we reached Sirius and wake me before Athena woke the rest of the crew."

Bartok hugged Anna from behind. "We were starving. The nutrient drip that supplied us with blood from the sleeping crew malfunctioned. Redfeather's blood clotting factor is much higher than expected and over the years. His blood clogged the system just like high cholesterol clogs human arteries. Nadia and I removed the monitors and drip system. We followed a maintenance bot into cryogenic hall three."

"There are thousands of bodies."

"We had to eat. We only killed one a day. We thawed them and drained them. We were going to wake you up when it was time."

"I can't believe you left such a mess. Why didn't you put the dead in the recycler?"

Nadia bared her fangs. "My sweet descendant, there was no point. We still intended to wake you and kill the crew as originally planned. Bartok and I would retire to chambers impervious to the light of Sirius and let you land the plane and wake the surviving colonists. You'd blame the slaughter on Redfeather and the crew."

Bartok walked to a cryogenic chamber and admired the sleeping woman. He activated the waking sequence. "Beautiful. She'll be delicious. Our plan will still work. Nadia and I will kill the crew and return you to suspended animation. We'll wake you just before we get close enough to Sirius for its solar rays to affect us. Smuggle us planet side at night. We'll convert you and the three of us will have an entire planet filled with colonists to feast upon. Dracula would be proud."

Anna said, "It could work, but even if it doesn't, I still have the ring containing your blood. If necessary, I'll drink it. Once on planet, I can cut myself and use my infected blood to reconstitute both of you."

"That's a long slow alternative, but we have as much time as we need."

Anna kissed the ring. "Stay in this room. During my next shift, I'll convince Hiroshi to stay behind. Take him first. After that, I'll pretend to be sick and get Leo alone in sickbay. We can pick them off one at a time."

Bartok said, "Warm living blood. I like that. The blood of the newly thawed is a bit cold for my taste."

***

Redfeather read the pilots' personnel files three times. Both were Eastern European, possibly of Magyar descent. They had military backgrounds and excelled as pilots. Extraordinary reaction times. There was nothing unusual there. They applied for the Methuselah Protocol and testing proved that their metabolisms were compatible. "Athena, show me all data on the Methuselah treatment."

"Jefferson, I've 62,851 files on Methuselah Protocol."

"Limit the files to ones specific to the treatment method."

"Six-thousand files."

Kendara said, "Athena, you aren't helping. Most of those files are publicity blurbs and propaganda. Let me think. I have it. Athena, show me a list of restricted files on the Methuselah Protocol."

"I have one restricted video file. To view this file, Captain Redfeather has to declare a pilot-related emergency. First Officer Kendara Kamaguchi must confirm the request, and security officer, Greg Flynn, must also verify. In the event one of these three people is deceased and the ship's computer confirms the death, the ship's computer may approve in place of the deceased officer. All three officers are alive and present."

"Captain Jefferson Redfeather speaking. I declare an emergency situation exists. The pilots have vanished. Athena show us the file."

Kendara and Greg confirmed Redfeather's request and Athena directed the crew's attention to a wall monitor."

"Good day. My name is Bradley Billings. I am the chief medical officer for the Interstellar Colonization Program. If you are watching this, there has been a failure with the Methuselah Protocol. One of two things has happened. If the pilots are deceased, this video will not help you. Request the ship's computer show you File 87564, Alternate Pilot Procedures. The crew will stand one year watches as pilots. View the details on the referenced file."

"The other potential failure is that the pilots are alive, but have abandoned their posts. Let me make this extremely clear. There is no Methuselah Protocol. The pilots are vampires, pure and simple. Take a moment. Yes, vampires are real. Vampirism, mystic or scientific, is a blood condition. Most of the stories are true. The disease is passed by an exchange of blood, but only a few people of Eastern European heritage are susceptible. Vampires are invisible to monitors and cameras. Their images don't appear in mirrors and they can become mist, wolves, bats, and who knows what else. Your pilots agreed to pilot your ship until it approaches its destination. In interstellar space, solar rays aren't strong enough to affect them and they can stay awake twenty-four seven."

"If things had happened properly, Bartok and Nadia would initiate the process to wake the crew, and depart the ship in specially designed escape pods. The pods are programmed to land them on a different planet in the Sirius solar system. Everyone would get what they want. Humanity gets a colony on New Philadelphia and Boris and Nadia get to live by feeding on the compatible life forms that exist on Sirius Six."

"Vampires are not inherently evil, but they want to survive, just like everyone else. They'll feed on you and the passengers to stay alive. In this worst case scenario, the crew must destroy Bartok and Nadia. The ship computer will be of no help. The vampires are invisible to the ship."

"Some old legends are true. Fire will kill them. You can disrupt their matrix by driving a sharp object into the center of their being. Traditionally, a wooden stake was used, but metal or plastic will suffice. The religious myths are nonsense. Holy water, communion wafers, and crosses are useless. Beheading will incapacitate the creatures, but burn the remains. Destroy the creatures completely. Even the smallest bit of flesh or a single drop of blood is enough for the vampire to survive. Complete regeneration in the presence of sufficient fresh blood has been documented."

"Three components of sunlight are visible light, ultraviolet light, and infrared light. The infrared component will destroy vampires. Matrix disrupting weapons and infrared flashlights are stored in compartment R14 in the crew's quarters. It is recommended that the crew work in pairs until any threat from rogue pilots has been eliminated."

"Can you believe this shit?" said Kendara. "What kind of idiot uses vampires to pilot spaceships?"

Hiroshi laughed. "The same idiots who believe in vampires."

Athena responded, "Public pressure for living pilots required a solution that was acceptable to the masses for the colonization program to achieve sufficient public support. The other option was for a small crew to stay awake for several years and wake successive replacement crews. An eight-hundred-year journey would require forty pairs serving twenty-five-year shifts. This was deemed unacceptable. The discovery of the vampire gene solved the problem. The Colonization Authority reached an understanding with vampires and rebranded the disease as the "Methuselah Protocol" for public consumption."

Redfeather said, "Thanks for nothing, Athena. Why didn't you tell us this before?"

"I did not have access to this data until you declared a pilot-related emergency."

"Fine," grumbled Redfeather. "Okay, stay in teams. Let's access our flashlights and stakes and go kill the vampires."

Kendara stood quickly, "Wait, where's Anna."

Athena responded, "Anna is in CH3. One more colonist storage chamber went offline six minutes ago.

Redfeather ordered, "Athena, do not open the door to CH3 for anyone except me. The vampires must be in the hall. Anna's a captive if they haven't already killed her."

Leo stayed at the table and poured himself a nutrient drink refill. "Really, Redfeather, vampires? Surely you could come up with something better than this for an emergency drill. You expect us to go charging around the ship playing Van Helsing carrying flashlights and spears. This is crap. Let's just finish cleaning up the dead, verify the ship's readiness, and go back to sleep until we reach Sirius."

"Athena is not programmed to joke."

Leo walked to the door. "Fine, if you say so. I won't participate in this farce. I'll clean sickbay and prepare our hibernation chambers. The rest of you have a good time playing cowboys and vampires. I'll have your chambers prepared when you're ready for your nap."

Redfeather said, "Anyone else in the mood to mutiny? I didn't think so. Stay together."

Redfeather led Kendara, Carl, Susanne, and Hiroshi to Storage Compartment R14. Hiroshi bounced a short plastic spear up and down to check the balance. The spear tip was hardwood reinforced with stainless steel or silver. Hiroshi laughed, "This is a little more old school than I expected. I'd hoped for a light sabre."

Redfeather said, "We can't hold a flashlight and fight with a spear at the same time. I plan to use the flashlights to force Bartok and Nadia into a corner. Carl and Susanne will keep them pinned in place with the infrared light and the other three of us will stab them."

Hiroshi said, "I've never stabbed a person."

Kendara smacked her spear against his. "None of us has. Bartok and Nadia have killed thousands of people. You can either be a fearless vampire slayer or you can be on the dinner menu."

Redfeather said, "Athena, don't let anyone, including Anna, out of CH3. Understood."

"Understood, Captain." Athena brought up a visual of Anna on the nearest monitor. She was seated on an empty cryogenic chamber. Her hands and feet were tied.

Carl asked, "Why did they tie her up instead of killing her?"

Kendara said, "Didn't you ever watch old movies? They want us to try and rescue her and they didn't have a railroad track."

"What's a railroad track?"

"If you don't get killed in the next few minutes, I'll show you later."

Carl and Suzanne clipped extra flashlights to their belts. Redfeather, Kendara, and Hiroshi carried a spear in one hand and a flashlight in the other. They lined up outside the door. Redfeather said, "On my command, Athena, open the door. Everyone, flashlights on. Carl and Suzanne enter first and the rest of us will follow. Athena, close the door immediately. Do not reopen it without command authorization codes. People, once inside, leave Anna tied up. Our priority is to find and destroy Bartok and Nadia."

Five infrared flashlights clicked on and bright red lights filled the corridor. Suzanne said, "We shouldn't be able to see infrared light."

"You can't," said Athena. "The light is tinted with red visible light so that you can see to aim it."

Redfeather stood to one side and motioned Suzanne and Carl into position. "Athena, open the door – NOW!"

Athena slammed the door closed behind Kendara two seconds later and the five people formed a circle facing outward and bathed the room in infrared light. The cloying stench from the unrecycled dead hit their lungs like a punch to the gut. Red beams played across the room.

Redfeather shouted, "Anna, where are Bartok and Nadia?"

"I don't know. Cut me loose."

"After we find them."

"I'm helpless. They'll kill me."

"If they wanted you dead, you'd be dead."

Anna screamed and cried. She begged. Suzanne left the group and ran to Anna. "Screw this. I'm cutting her loose."

Suzanne put down her flashlight and reached for the stiff knots binding Anna's hands. The slick plastic rope came loose at her first touch. Anna kicked her feet free and grabbed Suzanne's hands. "Thank you, dear."

"You're welcome. Take one of the flashlights. Help us find them."

Anna tightened her grip on Suzanne's hands. "I don't need a flashlight. I'm perfectly safe."

Suzanne tried to free her hands, but Anna squeezed harder, shifted her weight, wrapped her arms around Suzanne, and pulled her into a full embrace. Suzanne hugged her back and said, "Let me go, we must find the pilots."

Anna squeezed harder. "Don't worry. They'll find us."

Bartok congealed into human form behind Suzanne. He leaned close and licked her neck. Suzanne turned her head and screamed. Bartok said, "Thank you, Anna. Please be so kind as to disable her flashlights." He bit into Suzanne's throat and pulled her down behind the empty cryogenic chamber.

Suzanne's screams turned into a bubbling gurgle before going silent.

Redfeather approached the empty chamber and kicked the ropes to one side. Anna jumped over the chamber and grabbed his spear with both hands. "Stop, Redfeather. You don't understand."

Redfeather yelled to Kendara and Hiroshi, "Cover me with the infrared." He dropped his flashlight and grappled for control of his spear. He tried to jerk it from Anna's grip, but she was stronger than he expected. "Tell me what I don't understand."

"Athena said that you accessed the Methuselah Protocol failure video. You know that Nadia and Bartok are vampires. You mustn't hurt them. Vampires have coexisted with humanity since before people painted bison on cave walls. Nadia is my ancestor. She became a vampire before your people walked over the vanished land bridge from Asia to America."

Redfeather wrestled harder for the spear. "Changes nothing. An ancient evil is still evil."

He lifted one foot and kicked Anna in the chest. She fell over the empty chamber. She rolled to her feet and looked closely at her left hand. The golden ring with a ruby stone on her third finger was undamaged. She kissed it. "Bartok, a little help please."

Bartok flew at Redfeather. The vampire caught the spear's shaft and ripped it from Jefferson's grip. Carl and Kendara flanked the vampire and used the infrared lights to herd the creature against the nearest wall. His skin blackened and blistered. The flesh bubbled, melted, and dripped from ancient yellow bones. Bartok cowered and covered his face.

Redfeather said, "Kill him, Hiroshi. I'll keep Anna away from you and watch for Nadia."

Hiroshi poked and prodded the smoking creature. Kendara screamed. "Quick screwing around. For God's sake, impale that son of a bitch. I don't think he can shift while we've got him lit up. Stab him in the damn heart."

Hiroshi held the spear overhead with both hands, but before he could thrust, Nadia dropped from the ceiling like an avenging angel. She hit Hiroshi with her full weight and he crumpled like a paper doll. She rolled to the side. Carl hit her with an infrared beam. Her smoking flesh bubbled and blistered. She scuttled out of the light, dissolved into a mist, and vanished.

"Let her go. We'll find her later," said Redfeather. "First, we finish Bartok. Everyone, light him up."

Bartok sizzled like a steak on a hot skillet. His flesh melted like tallow and his bones exploded like flash powder with a loud whoosh.

Kendara said, "He's gone. There's no ash or even a stain."

Hiroshi groaned and sat against the wall. "I think she broke my collarbone."

Redfeather handed him two flashlights. We're going to find Nadia. Protect yourself."

Hiroshi pointed across the room. "Anna's trying to open the door."

Anna recited the emergency override code to Athena. Nadia assumed human form at her side. "Hurry, my child."

Carl, Redfeather, and Kendara ran toward the door. Redfeather screamed, "No, Athena, No. Don't open the door."

Athena said, "Emergency override code verified. Access granted." She opened the door.

Nadia shoved Anna aside and stepped into the open doorway. Leo stood facing her reciting the emergency override codes. He almost fell over from surprise when the door opened before he finished. He stumbled backward and clear liquid sloshed from the two large glass beakers. The cold liquid chilled his hands as it evaporated.

Nadia showed her fangs and snarled at Leo. He threw the contents of both beakers in her face. Nadia froze for a moment and Leo took a lighter from his belt, shoved it in Nadia's face, and clicked it three times.

It ignited on the third click and the ethyl alcohol exploded into flame. Leo covered his face. He screamed, "Burn, witch, burn."

Carl and Hiroshi restrained Anna. Four flashlights played across Nadia's burning body until nothing remained of the vampire.

Anna cried, "I hope you're happy. She was old before the first pyramid was built. She taught humans to hunt mastodons and fight sabre-toothed tigers. You should be ashamed."

"No, I feel proud, tired, and afraid, but mostly proud."

Kendara said, "Leo, I thought you didn't believe in vampires. I didn't expect you to help us."

"I didn't and I wasn't, but I watched the monitor and when Suzanne's throat exploded, I changed my mind. Fire is one of the things that kill vampires and I filled two beakers with ethyl alcohol and brought a lighter. I almost had a heart attack with the door opened before I finished saying the override codes."

Redfeather said, "First things first. Put Anna in a cryogenic chamber. Athena, don't reanimate her until I say so."

Carl and Kendara held her upper arms and marched her to an empty chamber. Anna didn't resist. She stepped into the chamber willingly. Kendara said, "Athena, activate chamber number CH3-34987.

The glass lid slid closed. Anna smiled and lifted her left hand to her mouth. She bit down on her ring and swallowed. Her body was flash-frozen in less than a second.

No one noticed the three drops of blood on her lips.

Why *Dracula* Rises Forever Undead
Denise Noe

When Bram Stoker wrote *Dracula*, the author created a character who would attain iconic status. Stoker's "undead" anti-hero rises forever no matter how often a stake is plunged through his heart. Not truly alive, Count Dracula never truly dies.

Abraham "Bram" Stoker was born in Dublin, Ireland, on November 8, 1847. His father was a civil servant, his mother, a charity worker and writer. Bram was close to his mother who regaled him with spooky stories. As an adult, Stoker worked in civil service and volunteered as *Dublin Evening Mail*'s drama critic.

In 1876, Stoker met actor Sir Henry Irving. The two became friends and Stoker became Irving's secretary/manager. Stoker married aspiring actress Florence Balcombe on December 4, 1878. Shortly after marrying, they moved to England to join Irving. Bram Stoker eventually became London's Lyceum Theater manager.

Stoker began writing. *Dracula* was published in 1897. Stoker wrote a play called *Dracula: Or, The Un-Dead: A Play in Prologue and Five Acts* based on the novel.

Stoker died in London on April 20, 1912. Two years later, Florence published a collection of his short stories that included "Dracula's Guest" which some believe was excised from the original *Dracula* manuscript.

The Story *Dracula* Told

Dracula is written in epistolary form. The story unfolds from diverse viewpoints. This allowed—and challenged—Stoker to express different voices. Reading *Dracula*, we read a potpourri of sources: Jonathan Harker's journal, letters between Mina Murray and Lucy Westenra, letters and telegrams from other characters, Dr. Seward's diary, Mina Murray's journal, newspaper clippings, medical reports, and ship logs. Through these varied voices, several plots and sub-plots develop, all brought together around the title figure.

Jonathan Harker has recently become an attorney. He leaves England for a trip to Transylvania to help Count Dracula acquire English properties. Of his journey, Jonathan writes, "We were leaving the West and entering the East." Jonathan writes about being among people "descended from Attila and the Huns" who seem to "believe every known superstition." When an elderly woman learns Jonathan will stay with Dracula, she insists Jonathan take a gift: a crucifix.

When Jonathan arrives at his destination, he meets Dracula, an elderly man "clean shaven save for a long white mustache, and clad in black from head to foot."

The Count appears hospitable, greeting, "Welcome to my house! Enter freely and of your own free will!"

Jonathan describes Dracula as having an "extraordinary pallor." The Count's oddest feature is "hairs in the centre of the palm" in each hand. Wolves howl; Dracula calls them "children of the night."

Dracula informs Jonathan he is free to explore the castle except its locked rooms. There is an echo of God telling Adam and Eve to partake of the fruit of every tree save one. Just as Eve was drawn to the Forbidden Fruit, Jonathan is drawn to locked rooms. Finding himself able to open a door despite its lock, he experiences "pleasure." Napping in the forbidden chamber, he is awakened by the appearance of three ladies with "voluptuous lips" and overcome by "a wicked, burning desire that they would kiss me with those red lips."

Suddenly Count Dracula is there, ordering the females away, exclaiming, "This man belongs to me!"

Jonathan is confused as Dracula tosses a bag to the women who exit with it. What is in that bag? Jonathan is horrified when he hears "a gasp and a low wail, as of a half smothered child." Soon Jonathan escapes the castle.

Count Dracula leaves for England on the ship, *Demeter*, taking with him several boxes containing Transylvanian soil.

Another plot strand concerns friends Mina Murray and Lucy Westenra. Mina is an assistant schoolmistress engaged to Jonathan Harker. Lucy is so attractive three men propose marriage to her in a single day! Arthur Holmwood, Dr. John Seward, and Quincey Morris are her suitors. Holmwood is a wealthy English aristocrat who will inherit his father's title of Lord Godalming. Not yet thirty years old, the distinguished Dr. Seward heads a "lunatic asylum." Quincey Morris is "an American from Texas." Lucy feels a tug toward each of her suitors but eventually accepts Arthur Holmwood's proposal.

At Dr. Seward's "asylum," a patient named Renfield eats live insects and spiders to acquire their "life force." Dr. Seward invents the term zoophagous for the "life-eating" patient.

Mina and Lucy are visiting in the seaside town of Whitby when the ship *Demeter* crashes ashore. The crew are missing; the dead captain strapped to the helm. The *Demeter* has a bizarre cargo: fifty boxes of soil from Transylvania. The only living being aboard is a big dog that immediately bounds ashore and races away.

In what seems a coincidence, Mina expresses concern that Lucy sleepwalks, an old habit of hers which obviously makes her vulnerable to predators, whether human, animal, or . . . "other." When Mina escorts Lucy home from a sleepwalking excursion to a cemetery, Mina is alarmed to see small wounds in Lucy's neck.

At about this time, Dr. Seward notices a change in the pathology of his most fascinating patient as Renfield loses interest in spiders but awaits the command of a mysterious man he calls "master."

Other developments occur. A sickly Jonathan Harker returns to Budapest. Mina travels to Budapest to join her fiancé. She is concerned when she finds him "so thin and pale and weak-looking" as well as harboring a terror of "great and terrible things."

After Lucy's sleepwalking misadventures, she falls ill. Her sickness comes and goes as she is sometimes her usual cheerful self, then suddenly falls into weakness and lethargy accompanied by extreme pallor. Dr. Seward examines Lucy but cannot diagnose her. He asks an old friend whom he knows to possess great knowledge, the learned Professor Van Helsing, to visit Lucy and see what he makes of her state.

Lucy is treated by methods both modern/medical and ancient/folkloric. She receives blood transfusions and, at Van Helsing's suggestion, her bedroom is draped with garlic, a substance believed to ward off vampires. However, the garlic is removed by Lucy's mother, Mrs. Westenra, who is unaware of their purpose. The young woman's condition deteriorates. She dies.

Or does she?

Soon after Lucy's demise, reports circulate of a strange lady walking at night. Children are most apt to report these sightings— and show tiny bite wounds on their own necks.

Van Helsing convinces Arthur Holmwood, Dr. Seward, and Quincey Morris that these sightings are of Lucy because Lucy is not truly dead but "un-dead." Van Helsing asks Seward if he believes the tiny holes in the children's necks were made by the same creature that made similar wounds in Lucy. "I suppose so," Seward replies and Van Helsing says it is "far, far worse": "They were made by Miss Lucy!" Van Helsing leads Dr. Seward to Lucy's coffin one night. It is empty! During daytime, they again visit the coffin. The professor "pulled back the dead lips" to show teeth "even sharper than before."

To give Lucy's soul rest, and to prevent the creation of more vampires, Van Helsing tells the others they must ensure Lucy's true death: They must drive a stake through the heart, cut the head off, and fill the mouth with garlic. Dr. Seward is appalled to learn of a plan that requires "mutilating the body of the woman whom I had loved." But he recognizes the truth that she is "un-dead." When Van

Helsing informs Arthur that the corpse of the woman he wanted to marry must be mutilated in the way just described, he is outraged: "What did that poor, sweet girl do that you should want to cast such dishonor on her grave?" However, Van Helsing convinces Arthur this is necessary so Lucy can be freed from vampirism.

The professor leads Dr. Seward, Arthur Holmwood, and Quincey Morris to Lucy's tomb. But she is not in the coffin. A figure approaches and Dr. Seward recalls, "We recognized the features of Lucy . . . [but] the sweetness was turned to adamantine, heartless cruelty and the innocence to voluptuous wantonness . . . . lips crimson with fresh blood" that streamed and "stained the purity of her death-robe." Seeing the four men, her eyes turn "unclean and full of hellfire."

Knowing that Lucy is indeed "un-dead," the group realizes they must bring about true death. They go to the tomb when she is in her coffin. Holmwood, who had been the fiancé of Lucy, plunges a stake through her heart. The vampire writhes in agony before collapsing into a normal corpse. Arthur kisses her. He and Morris leave. Van Helsing and Seward decapitate the body and put garlic inside the mouth of the disembodied head.

The group determines to find Dracula and destroy him. They are joined by Mina and Jonathan who, having wed in Budapest, return to England.

The group's efforts take on a special urgency when Dracula is discovered preying upon Mina. Seward writes, "His right hand gripped her by the back of the neck, forcing her face down on his bosom." Her white nightdress was smeared with blood while "his eyes flamed with devilish passion" and "her eyes were mad with terror." The men advance upon him, holding crucifixes before him, and Dracula changes into "faint vapor," escaping "under the door."

Lucy was made "un-dead." Can they save Mina from the same fate?

Vampires can only rest in homeland soil. The group discovers where the boxes of Transylvanian earth that Dracula uses as sanctuary are kept, They remove the dirt from the boxes and put sacramental wafers inside, making it impossible for Dracula to use them. With one remaining untouched box, Dracula flees to Transylvania. But he has bitten Mina who might turn vampire unless they destroy Dracula.

They pursue Dracula to his home. But before that, Seward researches Dracula's history, discovering he was "in life a most wonderful man," a soldier and statesman who possessed "learning beyond compare." A vampire's bite turned him into a monster.

The mission is accomplished and Dracula crumbles to dust. However, Morris Quincey is mortally wounded in the battle with Dracula and dies—but he dies knowing that Mina has been set free and is in no danger of becoming a vampire.

The story ends with an entry made in Jonathan's journal seven years after Dracula's destruction. The Hackers have a son named Quincey. The novel ends: "This boy will someday know what a brave and gallant woman his mother is. Already he knows her sweetness and loving care. Later on he will understand how some men so loved her, that they did dare much for her sake."

One of the wonders of *Dracula* is that it is, without strain, susceptible to many interpretations. Indeed, it is difficult to think of a novel that has a richer multiplicity of themes than this work that can easily be read as "about" morality, gender roles, sexuality, child abuse, alcoholism/addiction, diseases, colonialism, money, and/or aristocracy.

Real-Life Draculas?

Historical personages may have influenced Stoker. Vlad "the Impaler" Tepes and Countess Elizabeth "the Blood Countess" Báthory have been suggested as models.

Vlad III as the "real" Dracula was developed in the book *In Search of Dracula* by historians Radu Fluoresce and Raymond T. McNally. It took hold in the popular imagination although the link is disputed by experts. Walachia Prince Vlad Tepes III (1431-1476) was known for cruelty. Vlad was the second of four sons born to Vlad II Dracul. Thus, Vlad III was "Dracula" or "son of Dracul." The "Dracul" name came from the Latin word for *dragon* and got attached to his father's name when he became part of the "Order of the Dragon" created by Holy Roman Emperor Sigismund for the defense of Christian Europe against the Ottoman Empire.

Vlad habitually had enemies impaled. When someone is impaled, they are pierced by a sharpened stake and left to die "impaled" on that stake. Vlad III is reported to have made a practice of taking meals surrounded by impaled victims, sometimes even dipping his bread into their blood.

It is not known with certainty that Stoker's novel was linked to Vlad as there is nothing in the novelist's copious notes about this historical figure. Medieval history professor, Florin Curta, believes Stoker named his villain "Dracula" only because "in Wallachian language [it] means devil."

Hungarian Countess Elizabeth Báthory has also been suggested as a Dracula model. *Dracula Was A Woman* by Raymond T. McNally, a book about Báthory, makes that suggestion in its title. Báthory was born in 1560 and died in 1614 and is believed to have murdered hundreds of young women. Her uncle, Stephen Báthory, was Poland's king. In 1575 she married Count Ferencz Nádasdy. Four children were born during the marriage which ended with the Count's 1604 death. Although gossip about her abusing serf women circulated during her husband's lifetime, it was after his death that stories of her *murdering* became common. Hungary's King Matthias ordered an investigation. According to *Encyclopedia Britannica*, "After taking depositions from people living in the area surrounding her estate," investigators concluded she had "tortured and killed more than 600 girls with the assistance of her servants." She and the accused servants were arrested in 1609, tried in 1611. Three Báthory servants were executed for multiple murders while Báthory was ordered confined for life to a single room in her castle. She died a few years after her imprisonment.

Despite the parallels in bloodthirsty crimes, we cannot know with certainty that either Vlad Tepes III or Countess Elizabeth Báthory were used by Stoker as models for Count Dracula.

We *do* know that Stoker visited an English library in 1890 and examined William Wilkinson's *The Accounts of Principalities of Wallachia and Moldavia*. He visited the Whitby Museum where he studied several maps by which he drew a route from London to a mountain in Romania. Stoker also interviewed Royal Coast Guard workers about a ship called the *Dmitri* that had run aground a few years previously. Some reported that a black dog had run from the ship.

Death and Disease Dynamics

Stoker drew on vampire mythology in writing *Dracula*. The *Encyclopedia Britannica* relates, "Creatures with vampiric characteristics have appeared at least as far back as ancient Greece, where stories were told of creatures that attacked people in their sleep and drained their bodily fluids." Eastern Europe was a hotbed of vampire tales in the medieval period with the word "vampire" itself originating in that area. Sometimes the corpses of people suspected to be vampires were exhumed and it is likely certain normal aspects of decomposition like the continued growth of hair and fingernails after death reinforced vampire belief.

In pre-modern times, it was difficult to pinpoint death with certainty. Doctors might pronounce individuals dead when they were actually in a coma, in shock, or even just passed-out drunk. The seemingly miraculous return to life of such people might lead to the idea that they were "undead."

Fear of vampires led to practices like putting stakes through corpses and burying them facedown so they would be unable to rise from their graves.

Several illnesses, including porphyria, pellagra, rabies, cholera, tuberculosis, and syphilis, are associated with vampire belief.

Porphyria is genetic. "Their skin tightens and shrinks, and when this occurs around the mouth, the canine teeth appear more prominent, suggestive of fangs," author Rob Roy notes. "Discoloration of the skin also gives sufferers a very pale appearance and, fittingly, garlic exacerbates these symptoms, so it should be avoided at all costs."

Caused by a chemical imbalance, pellagra's symptoms include sensitivity to sunlight, pallor, and foul breath. The reddish color of urine in someone with pellagra may have led to suspicions they drank blood. There are in fact reports of pellagra sufferers drinking animal blood in (unconscious) attempts to replace chemicals missing from their bodies.

Real epidemics of pellagra and rabies (the latter from rabid wolves) may have contributed to the "Vampire Epidemic" in the 18th century, the century prior to Stoker's. Stanley Stepanic, a professor of Slavic languages and literature, observes that the Vampire Epidemic arose "after a case in Serbia in 1725 where people believed a vampire had appeared and caused illness" and "another case in 1726" led a "hysteria concerning vampires" to "spread through Eastern Europe and even parts of Western Europe." Just as the aforementioned symptoms of pellagra echo vampire characteristics, rabies victims avoid sunlight and are especially repulsed by strong odors (garlic is known for its strong odor).

Stoker's mother lived through a cholera epidemic as a teenager in the 1830s and likely told him about it. In 1873, Charlotte Thornley Stoker wrote a memoir entitled *Experiences of the Cholera in Ireland*. Tatiana Eva-Marie observes in "Infectious Disease in Bram Stoker's *Dracula*" that Victorian doctors subscribed to the theory of "miasmatism" which asserted "diseases like cholera were caused by 'bad air' emanating from rotting organic matter, poor hygiene, foul smells." Thus, Stoker writes of Harker repulsed by the Dracula castle's "pungent, acrid odor." The Count sometimes takes on the form of a mist.

By the time Stoker penned *Dracula*, the germ theory was edging out previous disease transmission theories. Before the female vampires are seen in *Dracula*, Harker sees "specks of dust dancing in the moonlight . . . they seemed to take dim phantom shapes." Indeed, germ theory can be seen when, just before Dracula attacks, Lucy notices "the air is full of specks, floating and circling in the draught from the window." Tatiana Eva-Marie writes, "The vampire famously hates garlic—and so does cholera; garlic is a natural antimicrobial, very efficient in fighting against bacteria; it is still routinely used today in the treatment of cholera in certain remote places."

Tuberculosis (TB) was called "consumption" because victims wasted away, or were "consumed," by it. TB was linked to vampirism because people close to an infected individual were apt to catch it. Many people thought the first infected person in a family drained the life force from others.

There was a concern with syphilis in Victorian society which might be reflected in *Dracula*. As Muscovits notes, "Syphilis has different stages, so death does not fall immediately, only after a certain latency period. Similarly, in *Dracula*, the victims of the vampire change gradually." Additionally, the way syphilis was viewed linked it to the "other." Muscovits comments, "Due to its fatal consequences and ignorance of its real nature, syphilis has been labelled as alien." The knowledge that syphilis was sexually transmitted connected it to licentiousness and guilt.

Stoker may have had a special reason to fear syphilis as some historians believed he not only contracted it but died of it.

Sexuality and Gender in *Dracula*

Understanding sex and gender in *Dracula* requires reviewing the well-known Victorian repression in which anything other than "missionary position" procreative marital sex was viewed as "perverted." Male homosexuality, even between consenting adults in private, was a crime, something underlined when author Oscar Wilde was convicted of homosexual activity in 1895 and sentenced to two years imprisonment at hard labor. Eszter

Muscovites wrote an essay, "The Threat of Otherness in Bram Stoker's *Dracula*," that suggested the vampire "carries in itself the anxiety in respect to homosexuality" and postulated "the act of bloodsucking is a metaphor for coitus as the canine tooth penetrates into the orifice on the neck." With the teeth representing a kind of sex organ, "The vampiric metamorphosis provides a kind of hermaphrodite status."

The vampire that creates other vampires in a sense gives birth, allowing males to "bear" and females to bear sans male impregnation.

Readers have seen strong sexual suggestions in *Dracula* since its publication. Perhaps the first clue we are given to Dracula's sexual corruption is in the description of him as having hairs in the palms of his hands. To the Victorian, hairy palms marked the masturbator.

When Dracula shoos his harem of female vampires away from Harker, proclaiming, "This man is mine!" he clearly indicates homosexual intentions.

Dracula attacks Lucy and Mina even as he intends to attack the men in their lives. "Your girls that you all love are mine already," Dracula gloats. "And through them you and others shall yet be mine —my creatures, to do my bidding and be my jackals when I want to feed." Muscovits also notes, "Vampires usually attack their victims regardless of their gender," linking them automatically to bisexuality. When Dracula forces Mina to suck blood from his own chest, he performs an act that resembles both fellatio and a child breastfeeding. That it is a woman sucking and a man giving suck subverts basic gender roles if seen as analogous to breastfeeding.

It is significant that the trio of female vampires in Dracula's harem and the vampiric Lucy attack children. Women are cross-culturally considered nurturers and protectors of children. However, the very fact that females give birth and usually spend more time with the young than males, means that children are usually harmed by females: the unwed teenager who bears in secret only to kill in panic; the mother suffering postpartum depression; the babysitter or nanny who loses her temper or is distracted at just the wrong moment. That the sex that nurtures is also apt to be the sex that harms is dramatized in *Dracula* by female vampires targeting children.

Generalizations about men and women are occasionally made by characters in the novel. One example is a rhetorical question Lucy asks in a letter to Mina: "Mina, why are men so noble when we women are so little worthy of them?" Some critics might see this as a male author projecting his own narcissism about his gender onto a female character. This critic sees it as something that realistically could be said by a woman since men often sacrifice themselves, even to the point of sacrificing their own lives, for the sake of the women they hold dear.

The "New Woman" was emerging when Stoker wrote *Dracula* and changing gender roles are directly addressed in the novel. In Mina Murray's journal, she makes a joke about how she and Lucy overate: "I believe we should have shocked the 'New Woman' with our appetites." Then Mina also pays tribute to the virtues of the male gender: "Men are more tolerant, bless them!" Then she mentions seeing Lucy sleeping and speculates: "Some of the 'New Women' writers will someday start an idea that men and women should be allowed to sleep together before proposing or accepting." Mina comments that things might get even stranger: "I suppose the 'New Woman' won't condescend in future to accept. She will do the proposing herself."

Mina believes she and other women possess a special psychological strength because they are female, writing, "We women have something of the mother in us that makes us rise above smaller matters when the mother spirit is invoked."

Good vs. Evil

Perhaps the most obvious theme in *Dracula* is good vs. evil. As Sarah L. Peters correctly asserts, "Stoker's Dracula is pure evil, repulsive and terrifying. He needs to take life, to end it or pervert it, and his foes are those who wish to preserve life. The roles in the story are rigid and clear-cut with definite lines between good and evil." One of the oddities of Count Dracula is that the reader cannot sympathize with him, a point underlined by Mina: "I suppose anyone ought to pity anything so hunted as the Count. That's just it: this Thing is not human—not even beast. To read Dr. Seward's account of poor Lucy's death, and what followed, is enough to dry up the springs of pity in one's heart."

This battle between good and evil is made all the more necessary by the power that the evil figure has to transform good beings into evil ones. The bite of the vampire does not "just" endanger life but, perhaps even more ominously, endangers morality. Indeed, that any human being, however virtuous, can be made evil by the vampire's bite is perhaps the most terrifying aspect of the vampire mythology.

Science vs. Superstition, Rationality vs. Faith

The 19th century was a period of extraordinary scientific progress: John Dalton published atomic theory (the concept that matter is made of particles so tiny they are invisible); Dmitri Mendeleev formulated the Periodic Table; James Clerk Maxwell proved light is an electromagnetic wave; Marie Curie discovered radium and polonium; Louis Pasteur proved microscopic organisms caused disease and invented pasteurization to stop bacterial contamination; Michael Faraday invented the dynamo; Samuel Morse invented the electric telegraph; and Alexander Graham Bell invented the telephone. In 1859, *The Origin of the Species* by Charles Darwin was published. Darwin's even more controversial *The Descent of Man* was published in 1871.

Accompanying scientific progress, and especially the controversial theory of evolution, was fear science would become a new dogmatism with a rigid "scientism" erasing the traditions that had developed over thousands of years. Perhaps this is why there was much interest in the occult.

Dracula reflects tension between science and superstition, or faith. It is similar to two other classics the era produced in seeing dangers in science. *Frankenstein* by Mary Shelley and *The Strange Case of Dr. Jekyll and Mr. Hyde* by Robert Louis Stevenson both focused on scientific experiments gone awry. No scientific experiment leads to Dracula. Rather, scientific methods are unable to defeat the vampire.

A writer observed on the *Monsters & Madness* website, "Science and pseudoscience figure prominently in *Dracula* because they reflect the confusion that Victorians felt about the mysteries of the modern world."

Dracula suggests we cannot totally rely on science but must retain and respect ancient ways. As *Literary Devices* avers, modern medical science through blood transfusions cannot save Lucy's life. After science fails and she becomes a vampire, those who care about her turn to "knowledge of traditions" to free her and bring about true death. Folkloric wisdom also leads to true death for Count Dracula. As the *Monsters & Madness* writer observes, these Victorian characters realize "supernatural means need to be used to counteract supernatural forces."

Kaitlin Blanchard suggests in an essay that a theme in *Dracula* is "science and superstition—or less pejoratively, faith—is not one of binary opposites." Blanchard believes Stoker sees science "as the evolutionary successor" to "faith-based belief." Blanchard sees *Dracula* as influenced by Charles Darwin and the theory of evolution. She notes how Renfield "methodically consumes life." Blanchard concludes, "The horrifying prospect that man can revert to beast, or worse, that beast can masquerade as man, is at the heart of *Dracula*'s power to terrify." Blanchard sees a hopefulness in *Dracula*. Its hero, Van Helsing, makes use of both science and superstition. Thus, "Stoker's intent [is] to illustrate the ability of two apparently dissimilar belief system to co-exist."

Privilege and Oppression, Wealth and Poverty

Literary Devices comments, "The power of money is another major theme of the novel." Dracula does not acquire English property or travel through supernatural means but through money. Money's role is underlined when Harker is in the castle and discovers heaps of gold.

Dracula can be viewed as symbolic of a corrupt wealthy ancient regime. The aristocrat, with his inherited wealth made ever greater through the work of his underlings, can be seen as feeding off the labor of the impoverished peasants much as the vampire feeds off the blood of the living.

In "The Economics of Dracula," Peter C. Earle points to Dracula's model, Vlad the Impaler, as symbolizing how money can be used for evil and how those who have it can victimize those who do not. Vlad waged a "war on poverty" that was a war on the poor. He invited the poor and disabled to a designated area for a feast. A feast was indeed prepared and many beggars and disabled attended it. The ruler asked, "Do you want to be without cares, lacking nothing in the world?" Of course they answered affirmatively. Vlad had the hall boarded up and set afire.

In "Why Count Dracula is always rich," Scott Grant argues Dracula is wealthy precisely because "he lives forever." Grant elaborates, "If you lived forever, you would be rich too. Given enough time and even a frugal rate of interest, your assets would grow into an immense fortune" as "simple saving and compounding over a long period of time is an astoundingly powerful tool." Grant believes that since people cannot live for hundreds of years, we "create organizations that do."

West to East, East to West

Conflict between Western and Eastern Europe is highlighted in *Dracula*.

First, Englishman Harker travels to Eastern Europe; then Transylvanian Count Dracula travels to England. Harker's mood becomes one of uncertainty, even confusion. Transylvanians offer gifts Harker finds of "an odd and varied kind." The logical, rational Western

European way is exemplified to Harker by a practical Eastern failing: "The further East you go the more unpunctual are the trains."

A *UK Essays* writer believes Stoker made his monster Transylvanian due to the writer's "unfavorable view of the East." Dracula's eventual defeat demonstrates Stoker's "favoritism" to Western Europe.

Joe Spillaine observes that England (and by extension Western Europe generally) symbolizes "rationality" with "rules and regulations" while the East remains governed by "magic" and superstition.

When the vampire travels to England, he symbolizes a fear that 19th century England could be in a sense "invaded" by Eastern Europeans. *Literary Devices* states, "Fear of outsiders entering one's country and causing havoc is another major theme of the novel."

Dracula Staked, Dracula Rising

Since its publication, *Dracula* has never been out of print. Dracula routinely appears in serious horror and in horror-comedy. He returns regardless of how often his heart is staked.

Dracula represents so much that is basic: sexual yearnings and sexual violence, disease transmission, the abuse cycle, the power of wealth turned, the fear of the "other." Dracula haunts us, Dracula terrifies us, Dracula fascinates us because Dracula is what we fear we could become . . . or are.

Works Cited
Barker, J.D.; Stoker, Dacre. "Bram Stoker Claimed That Parts of *Dracula* Were Real. Here's What We Know About the Story Behind the Novel." *Time*. Oct. 3, 2018.
Blanchard, Kaitlin. "Beyond Belief: The Role of Science and Modernity."
http://engl358dracula.pbworks.com/w/page/18970608/Beyond%20Belief%3A%20The%20Role%20of%20Science%20and%20Modernity#:~:text=At%20a%20time%20when

%20modernity,and%20superstitions%20reared%20its%20head.

"Conflicts Between East and West in Dracula." https://us.ukessays.com/essays/english-literature/conflicts-between-east-and-west-in-dracula-english-literature-essay.php#:~:text=In%20Dracula%2C%20Bram%20Stokers%20shows,the%20exotic%20and%20alienated%20Eastern.

Dang, Duy. "A Disease with a Bite: Vampirism and Infection Theories in Bram Stoker's *Dracula*." *Digital Commons*. April 2013.

"Dracula." *BramStoker.org*.

"Dracula." *Encyclopedia Britannica*.

"Dracula." *SparkNotes*.

"'Dracula' by Bram Stoker." Medium. https://medium.com/@kon7kour/dracula-by-bram-stoker-48ec30857643

"Dracula Themes." *Literary Devices*.

Earle, Peter C. "The Economics of Dracula." American Institute for Economic Research." Oct. 31, 2018.

Eva-Marie, Tatiana. "Infectious Disease in Bram Stoker's *Dracula*." *Shrine Magazine*.

Grant, Scott. "Why Count Dracula is always rich." *Ponte Vedra Recorder*. Jan. 3, 2019.

Kelly, Jane. "How the Spread of Disease Juiced the Lore of Vampires into Pandemic Proportions." *UVA Today*. Oct. 28, 2020.

Lallanilla, Marc; McKelvie, Callum. "Vlad the Impaler: The Real Dracula." *Live Science*. Dec. 15. 2021.

Lambert, Tim. "Science and Technology in the 19th Century." https://localhistories.org/science-and-technology-in-the-19th-century/

Peters, Sarah L. "Repulsive to Romantice: The Evolution of Bram Stoker's *Dracula*."

Roy, Rob. "Dracula's Disease." *New Scientist*. Feb. 23, 2011.

"Science and Pseudoscience in Dracula." Monsters & Madness: Secret Lives in Victorian Literature." https://blogs.dickinson.edu/secretlives/2017/11/13/scie

nce-and-pseudoscience-in-dracula/#:~:text=Overall%2C%20science%20is%20the%20first,a%20place%20in%20the%20world.

Spillane, Joe. "Dracula: East vs. West." https://www.writing.com/main/view_item/item_id/1453312-Dracula-East-vs-West

Stepanic, Stanley. "The Rise of the Vampire: How Diseases May Have Led To Dracula." *The Conversation.* 10/23/2021.

Stoker, Bram. *Dracula.* Black & White Classics. 2014.

www.ingramcontent.com/pod-product-compliance
Lightning Source LLC
LaVergne TN
LVHW012053070526
838201LV00083B/4518